THE QUEEN'S HIDDEN LEGACY

—A PREQUEL NOVELLA—

SHONNA SLAYTON

AMARETTO PRESS

To Morag

AUTHOR NOTE

I never planned to write a prequel for the River Kelpie Series. But after *Rise of the Kelpies* came out, I realized that I needed more details about the history of the Kelpie Wars, at least as far as they pertained to this particular king and queen before I wrote the sequel. So, I went backward to go forward and decided to take you along for the ride.

Because the series has some big twists and turns, the order you read will affect your expectations and give a spoiler or two. So if you like to read in publication order, start with *Rise of the Kelpies*. If you like story order, start with this prequel.

PRONUNCIATION GUIDE: If you're wondering about how to pronounce the King and Queen's names, know that Queen Cadha has a tricky name as it is an old name and not often used today. As best I could determine, the traditional pronunciation is *Ka-ya* but modern pronunciation guides incude *Ka-dha or Kay-da*. In my head, I say *Ka-dha*. King Seamus is pronounced *SHAY-mus*.

GLOSSARY

This story is set in a land inspired by Celtic folklore. Characters use vocabulary such as:

- **Aye** for yes
- **Nae** for no
- **didnae** for did not (past tense)
- **dinnae** for do not (present tense)
- **cannae** for can not
- **wasnae** for was not
- **mustnae** for must not

(Seeing the pattern?)

- **bairns** for babies and young children
- **braw:** good, fine
- **burn:** creek
- **holloway:** a sunken lane
- ye **ken** for you know
- **och** as an interjection, like "Oh!"

CHAPTER 1
QUEEN CADHA

Morag flew through the drafty stone corridor of the royal quarters, humming a tune to hide the irritation she was feeling. She smoothed the annoyance from her face as she chased down the royal nanny. The woman held one ten-day-old baby in each arm, the twins freshly bathed, ready for sleep. The nanny knew Morag was behind her, but she bustled along anyway, gleeful that she could outpace a palace fairy, even if the fairy had an injured wing.

When the nanny had to pause and open the queen's sitting-room door, Morag caught up to her.

"Why hello, sunshine and starlight." Morag forced her way past the nanny's protective stance, extending her hands for the wee prince and princess to grasp. "Have you been fair goodly ones for your mother today?"

The nanny frowned and pulled the twins away from Morag. "The princess has a right set of lungs on her. We all tried to keep the queen from hearing too much during her daily rest, but you know how she is."

Morag straightened to her full height, as tall as the nanny's waist, and followed the crotchety woman through the sitting room, still trying to attract the babies' attention. She beamed when the prince squeezed her finger, however accidentally at his age. "Och, he's a braw lad, this one. We could call him Fergus. A strong name like that and no one will tease him about his unfortunate birthmark." *Although longer hair would also take care of that.*

The warmth of the room struck Morag as she entered the queen's bedroom. A young attendant carefully stoked the glowing peat fire on the hearth. The fire served to ward off the autumn chill and warm the ailing queen, but it left a strong earthy scent hanging in the air.

The tapestries covering the stone walls here were softer and more delicate than those in the corridors, telling tales of love rather than battle. Near the window, a special floor-to-ceiling tapestry of a regal unicorn standing proudly and unchallenged dominated the room.

Heavy drapes in a deep evergreen fabric framed the window looking out over the low, setting sun. The queen's four-poster bed, a grand structure of carved mahogany, centered the room, its hangings embroidered with the royal crest and trimmed with thick braided cord. A large oak cradle waited at the foot of the bed, lined with soft linens and a gossamer veil to protect the infants from drafts. Not that they spent much time sequestered there, as the queen preferred the twins at her side.

Morag broke away from the overprotective nanny and stood near the cradle. "Cadha, you should call the lad Callum. And then the lass can be Cara. Peace and friendship. And your names would alliterate."

The weary queen finished brushing the ends of her long auburn hair before placing her silver brush on the bedside table. She pushed herself up, leaning against the plush headboard as she readied herself to hold her babies. She set her blue eyes firmly on Morag. "Nae, Morag, you'll not hear their names from me. Not until their naming ceremony. What would the king say?" She took several shallow breaths before reaching for her twins. "It'll be soon enough, and you and the entire kingdom will learn their names."

"As you wish. But if you don't mind me suggesting, Ian and Iona are nice names as well. Would be lovely for twins, both acknowledging divine blessing."

Cadha ignored Morag and kissed each little head. "And how did the day go today?"

Undaunted that her suggestions were rebuffed, Morag pivoted to give her account. "The rivermen are busy as ever upstream on the secret project your husband has them on. But the watchmen saw several kelpies in the water, prowling about near the bridge. They've added more guards to the patrols to watch for those water horses."

The nanny shot Morag a withering look before she spoke sharply. "Enough of that. Let the queen focus on getting her strength back. I want no more relapses of that lung disease." With a practiced motion, she adjusted the thick blankets around Cadha, tucking them in with care that spoke of a deep, if stoic, affection.

Cadha and Morag exchanged a look over the nanny's head. The woman muttered as she flitted about the room tidying what didn't need to be tidied. She hovered near the queen's vanity, straightening creams and perfumes that the queen hadn't used in months.

Queen Cadha still had her lung disease, and they all knew that she wasn't recovering from it. But if pretending helped the nanny carry on through her duties with the children, they would allow her the fiction.

"Morag, off you go to dinner before you're missed. We'll talk more tomorrow, I promise." The queen reached out to take Morag's hand. "Thank you for being my eyes and ears. I'd be as forgotten as an old mop if it weren't for you. Check in with Solly to make sure she's still happy to keep tending my garden, even though I haven't been able to take the bairns there yet. And tell Mavis I miss her visits, but I understand how busy she is."

"Aye. But before I go, you ought to know there have been developments." She glanced at the nanny, wishing she would leave. "It's been noticed that supplies have been disappearing from the kitchen. Osario is making a fuss about it. He's got an ambitious young guard patrolling with him and searching for clues. There'll be a right ruckus when they find who's taking those supplies."

The queen looked distracted, snuggling noses with the prince and princess, but Morag knew her well enough to not feel slighted. The queen was paying close attention. As was the nanny, so Morag was careful with her words.

"Anything else that I should know about?" Cadha asked, her gaze momentarily shifting from her children to Morag.

Morag nodded thoughtfully. "Aye, a few things worth noting. First, there's talk among the townsfolk of a strange figure seen at dusk by the river. Some say he's a wandering bard, others claim it's a kelpie in human guise. Also, the blacksmith's apprentice has gone missing, and rumor has it he had a quarrel with his master over the quality of steel being forged for the guards. And finally, Solly's been complaining about holes in the garden."

"Holes?"

"Holes."

"I can see how that would vex Solly." The queen waved her hand. "I'm sure she'll have it figured out by week's end." Cadha shifted the squirming princess. "What about this bard? Any description? Outstanding features?"

"Descriptions vary, but most agree on a few points. He's cloaked, with a wide-brimmed hat shadowing his face. No one's seen him up close, but there's an air about him that makes people suspicious."

The queen leaned forward, her interest clearly piqued. "Does this wide-brimmed hat hold a flower?"

"Dinnae ken. I'll find out."

"Do. Thank you, Morag." The queen looked out the window at the river. "Take care who you ask. Until we learn friend or foe, I don't want anyone knowing that I'm doing anything but tending me bairns." She glanced back at Morag, her eyes conveying the seriousness of the situation.

"Not even Solly will suspect, and you know how sneaky she is at getting information out of me. I will stand strong." With a final glare at the nanny, Morag left the room, wondering what the woman had gleaned from their conversation.

CHAPTER 2
THIEF BUSINESS

The rafters in the castle were a network of dark wooden beams, aged and weathered, and used by the fairies to travel quietly and mostly unnoticed. Morag used them now to fly silently above the servants, who were taking empty trays and pots back to the kitchens.

The other palace fairies were already in the great hall. Mavis and Marisol (who preferred to go by Solly) also wore their wool kirtles, long dresses with generous pockets decorated with silver embroidery. Mavis in moss green, Marisol in mauve, and Morag in dull tan.

Below, the great hall was filled with long, rough-hewn wooden tables and benches. The stone floor, worn smooth over the years, gleamed in the orange glow of the fire and candle flames. Outside the castle, the night winds howled, indicating another shift in the weather.

Morag's right wing throbbed after a long day, and she was grateful for the rest. Their perch, though unobtrusive to the humans below, placed them near the warmth of the hearth and had become a welcome snug over the years.

"You're late. Is all well?" Mavis asked as Morag settled in. Dinner was almost over, and the hall lads had cleared the tables.

The kitchen maids were now coming in with dessert. The great hall, usually loud with the clatter of plates and hum of conversation, held a somber tone tonight. The usual abundance of fresh fish and roasted game had dwindled, replaced with more modest fare of pottage and oat cakes for most meals. A sign of the strain the Kelpie Wars had put on the kingdom's resources as the water horses terrorized trade along the River Tarner.

"The queen is with her bairns, so aye." Morag gave a tired smile. "All is well."

"*Och,* today might be the day," Solly whispered as she nudged Morag and pointed toward the arched door. Solly leaned forward expectantly, elbows on knees, but Morag did not share her sense of eagerness.

A pretty maid entered, balancing a large tray of butter tarts, her cheeks flushed from the heat of the ovens. A young soldier was about to cut in front of her, his eyes focused on adjusting the claymore sword on his belt. The collision was inevitable.

Daria's tray of butter tarts flew into the air, landing with a crash that echoed around the great hall. The soldier blushed, apologizing profusely, while Daria stood frozen in shock. A smattering of laughter spread through the room, and the two shared an embarrassed smile and flustered apologies.

Solly clasped her hands together. "There. Now, they've met."

"You didn't interfere, did you, Solly?" Morag asked.

The scene was charmingly human, one of many budding romances the fairies had witnessed over the years, and a welcome distraction amidst the throes of the Kelpie Wars. But it did little to appease the unease gnawing at Morag's insides.

"Didnae have to," Solly said, shaking her curly head. "Besides, Mavis predicted it weeks ago."

Mavis, with a knowing look, leaned over to talk around Solly. "'Twasn't difficult. I've caught the maid sneaking glances at the lad since he arrived with the latest recruits. And see on his wrist? He's wearing the leather cord that she braided. All the maids are making tokens for the soldiers to give them courage, and he just *happened* to get the one woven by her hand."

Morag let the other two discuss young love while her gaze wandered elsewhere. Tensions in Kingston were already high because of an uptick in missing townsfolk, but tonight, something felt extra amiss. The queen would want to know what.

"Morag, where is your key?" Solly pointed her finger accusingly.

"It's right here." Morag's hand flew instinctively to her neck, fingers fumbling for the comforting weight of the key on its string. But she patted her woolen kirtle in vain. A familiar wave of frustration washed over her, and she dodged Solly's accusing gaze.

"I told you we shouldn't let her have one, Mavis. If she ever had a chance to use it, it would be lost anyway."

Mavis sighed, and Morag steeled herself for a lecture. Mavis, the oldest of them, often took charge and was prone to lecture a paragraph too long. Her brown hair was heavily highlighted with silver strands, which she said were caused by the other two's bickering.

"What's worrying you now?" Mavis asked instead. Her brilliant eyes, filled with concern, locked onto Morag. "You haven't been yourself since the queen fell so ill after the birth. If this war lasts much longer, you'll have lost everything in your pockets."

Solly let out a burst of air, her irritation clear, despite knowing that Morag wasn't intentionally misplacing objects. Solly just liked her opinions to be known, as if they were ever in question.

This new quirk in Morag's magic, which had crept up after her injury, refused to mend as she'd hoped. Morag was tiring of the problem as much as Solly was. It was bad enough she couldn't fly the way she used to, but this irregular, unpredictable misplacing of objects made her a liability when her role required dependability and predictability. Solly was not wrong to be irritable.

"Mavis, you should use your time mirror to find out when it went missing," Solly pressed. "That'll help Morag find it." Solly was always trying to get Mavis to look into the past, but Mavis used her mirror sparingly.

"Nae," Mavis said. "The mirror 'tis not something we can rely upon, much like Morag's pockets as of late."

"But Mavis..."

While Solly expounded on the benefits of magic mirrors, Morag turned away and focused on the disconcerting scene below. "I'm sensing something," she interrupted.

"Of course you are." Solly huffed. "You'll go off *sensing* for something." She wiggled her fingers when she said the word *sensing*. "While me and Mavis do all the work."

"Hush, Solly, and let her concentrate. She might find her key while she's at it."

The other palace fairies relied on observation, but Morag was gifted with something more. A deeper intuition, an ability to perceive the motivations of those around her. Tonight, that sense prickled.

Someone down below was trying very hard not to think about doing something they shouldn't. If only Morag could home in on the guilty conscience...

A merchant with many rings on his fingers leaned toward an official with shifty eyes and whispered, "When a town has a dragon, they sacrifice a young girl to it once a year and get on with their lives. I don't know why we can't do the same thing with the kelpies. If they crave human flesh, let's work out an agreement so there's no more wondering who it's going to be next?"

The official nodded. "It's only one soul, and it could be a lass or a laddie. That should keep the lasses from complaining that the sacrifice always has to be one of them." He chuckled before taking a swig from his tankard. "I'll speak with King Seamus again. See if we cannae get this kelpie problem straightened out one way or another."

Lord Ewan. Morag frowned and continued scanning the people below, her gaze finally landing on Senna, the archivist's teenage daughter. She was a young woman with fiery red hair and fierce determination in her eyes. Young Senna was a lass of few words, often lost in thought, so it was especially noticeable now that her gaze shifted, and her foot twitched nonstop under the table.

Och, lass, you give yourself away too readily.

As the laughter subsided and the remainder of the butter tarts were being served, Senna got up and furtively slipped out of the room.

Morag rose to follow.

"Now where are you—" Solly started to say loudly, but stopped when Morag frowned at her. No need to announce her movements to the entire hall.

Flying above, Morag caught up to Senna as she sneaked through the halls, her footfalls surprisingly silent on the stone floors. Morag followed, high up in the dark spaces in the rafters, keeping out of sight and maintaining a keen eye on the young lass.

Senna continued her stealthy path into the kitchen, now empty of all but the busy dishwashers focused on finishing their work for the night. They splashed in the sudsy water, clanking the tin plates and iron pots, seemingly oblivious to Senna walking in behind them.

The kitchen's low doorway caused Morag a moment's pause, but she entered unnoticed before tucking herself up behind the hanging pots to continue her surveillance.

Senna paused at the closed door into the storeroom. Her gaze scanned the backs of the dishwashers before she opened the door and slipped inside. The dim, cool room was filled with stacks of grain, barrels of salted meat, and rounds of cheese—barely the sustenance the castle needed to survive the recent bout of attacks.

With care, Senna filled a sack with day-old bread and cheese. The lass paused for a long moment before selecting a few other random packages from the storeroom. She appeared to be in no hurry.

Morag bit her lip, with her gaze now focused on the kitchen doorway. The castle was under strict rationing; any pilfering, no matter how small, would be dealt with harshly. The consequences could be severe, even for someone like Senna, who was allowed certain liberties because of her father's position.

The sound of heavy footfalls echoed in the corridor, getting louder. Morag recognized the rhythmic clatter of chain mail. Osario, the king's personal guard, along with a younger junior guard, was approaching. Fast. Osario was a known stickler for the rules, and Senna was about to get caught in the act. What would the lass's excuse be?

Osario burst into the kitchen with the wiry, sandy-haired guard at his heels. The dishwashers stopped their work, turning with mouths agape.

He looked up and glared at Morag as if to say, What are you doing here?

Morag glared back at him. *Och, the man is too observant for his own good. If he was going to make a scene, he ought to leave me out of it.* He stopped her from speaking with a raised hand and marched directly to the storeroom. He filled the doorway, his stern gaze focused on Senna. Senna, a young lass, but nearly a woman, would not be shown mercy. She was old enough to know better.

The dishwashers followed Osario's every move. Soapy water dripped from stilled hands and puddled on the floor. No one wanted to be the object of Osario's wrath, but he was hard to look away from.

"I told you it were her," the sandy-haired guard crowed. He sneered at Senna.

"Ye ken it's forbidden, Senna," Osario's voice was as hard as the iron chain mail he wore. Senna's gaze flicked to the other guard, a smug look on his face as he leaned against a barrel, arms crossed over his chest.

Senna was a vision of defiance, her chin raised, her hazel eyes steady despite her predicament. "Those bairns in the town need it more than we do here at the castle. They've naught but scraps," Senna protested, her voice steady.

"You've no right to make that decision," Osario retorted, his hand closing around the sack. "There's mouths enough to feed here, too. Your actions compromise the castle's resources."

"Ye ken how much we have?" She held onto the sack and jerked her chin toward the shelves. "Those wee'uns are starvin'." Senna's voice cracked, her frustration clear. But her plea seemed to bounce off Osario's steely exterior.

The guard with Osario shifted his position and spoke as if he had authority. "We could send those orphans to the kelpies and be done with the war straightaway. They'll not be hungry, and the kelpies be full and leave us alone. Everyone wins."

This one's been listening to Lord Ewan and his ilk. Ewan owned the new mill, the blacksmith, and used to control most of the trade on the Tarner until the Kelpie Wars started. He cared more about his interests than those of the kingdom. Ironic, since it was his nephew who allowed most of the kelpie herd to escape in the first place. When a kelpie's magical bridle is replaced with one made from kingdom silver, it becomes tame and will work for the king. But if the royal bridle is removed, the kelpie is no longer subdued and can escape back to the river. It won't be able to transform out of its horse form, but it will no longer be under submission. Lord Ewan's nephew had removed the king's bridles at the end of one day and then in the morning had started replacing them with the kelpies' own magical bridles before he was stopped by the stablemaster, screaming, "You fool!" For he knew the kelpies had waited, hoping to get their magic bridles back from the witless stable hand. The stablemaster was killed when the kelpies dragged him to the river while making their escape.

Senna shot a look at the junior guard that would freeze the mightiest river midflow. "Would that you were a wee bairn, then you would ken different. We ought to send you out to the kelpies."

Osario's gaze hardened. "Senna, you cannae be workin' in the castle if you cannae show respect and follow the rules. You're dismissed."

Morag sucked in a breath as she waited for Senna's response.

"That's all?" the junior guard rose to his full height. "The likes of her is trouble. Best deal with her right away—the hole, wouldn't you say?"

Osario ignored the man, his focus strictly on Senna.

"But my da—"

"Your da cannae save you from your own actions, lass. You're lucky I'm only dismissing you and not sending you to the dungeons." Osario's voice turned colder. "Be gone by morn. I'll arrange it so the guard will grant you passage over the main bridge to town."

Senna's shoulders slumped, but she quickly squared them, lifting her chin. "Aye," she said, her voice barely above a whisper. "I'll go. But ye ken deep down that I needed to do this."

As Senna squeezed past Osario and left the storeroom, Morag tucked herself farther out of sight. Both Senna and Osario were correct. The orphans needed taking care of and the provisions were needed at the castle to keep up the soldiers' strength. Each of them offered a decent argument.

Wanting to check on Senna's next move, Morag emerged from her hiding place and cast a glare Osario's way. He lifted his hands in exasperation, but she ignored him and shot out of the kitchen.

"You best not meddle," he called after her in warning.

The young guard with him snickered. Morag refrained from responding to either. Osario knew she would do exactly what she was sent to do, and the young guard would learn one day not to be so flippant about other people's lives.

CHAPTER 3

LORD EWAN

That brief interaction with Osario and the guard cost her. The hallway was empty. *Where would Senna go next?* Morag navigated the dimly lit passageways, searching after the lass in vain. Down the business wing, a thin beam of light spilled out of the council chamber and into the hall, along with tense voices.

Morag forgot about Senna and quietly made her way to this new distraction. She landed on the ground and carefully peeked through the partially open door. The king and several of his advisers met around a large rectangular table, their faces grim. One large map of the kingdom lay out, the king's fingers tracing the river that snaked through the landscape. His large signet ring, his symbol of power, glinted in the light.

"We must fortify the bridges," one adviser insisted. "If they fall, we'll have no safe passage from one side of the kingdom to the other."

"And what of the villages along the river?" another countered. "We can't leave them defenseless. We need a strategy to protect our people, not just our infrastructure."

Morag's heart sank as she listened. The kelpies' aggression was pushing the kingdom to its limits and forcing difficult decisions with no simple answers. In the past, the kelpies were content to trick humans to come to them, acting like docile horses standing innocently near the river, tempting for children to ride and farmers to take. Wearing a bridle, a kelpie looked as tame as any village horse. But once the kelpie had a rider, it would turn on the unsuspecting person, drowning them in the river before eating them.

"We all know there is another solution. The people are calling for it. If you would just listen to Lord Ewan—"

The adviser looked up, noticed the open door, and frowned. He strode forward, and Morag pressed back against the wall, out of sight. He slammed the door closed.

The voices were now too muffled for Morag to hear, even with her ear pressed against the wood. Thwarted again, she renewed her effort to find Senna.

As she approached the corner at the end of the hall, she nearly collided with Lord Ewan himself as he stepped out from a concealed doorway where he'd been lurking. His eyes, sharp and calculating, fixed on her with an unsettling intensity.

"Good evening, Morag," he said, his voice dripping with feigned politeness that did little to mask his disdain. "You seem to be in quite a hurry. Perhaps fleeing from some fairy mischief?"

Morag steadied herself, her wings fluttering slightly. "Nae, Lord Ewan. Just attending to the queen's needs, as always."

"Ah, yes, the queen and her precious fairies." Lord Ewan stepped closer, his presence imposing. "I've noticed your frequent visits to the queen's chamber. Tell me, what counsel do you offer her in these trying times?"

His words carried an unspoken accusation, and a chill ran through her. She knew Lord Ewan's stance on the kelpie situation and his skepticism toward the fairies.

"If you imply that we're a threat, you're mistaken," Morag replied, her voice firm. "Our loyalty lies with the queen, and any counsel we give her is for her guidance alone."

"Guidance," he echoed mockingly. "And yet, the castle whispers of strange happenings. Disappearances. Unexplained events. One can't help but wonder if fairy *guidance* is part of the cause. If, perhaps, fairy guidance is what's standing in the way of reason."

Morag refused to engage the way Ewan wanted her to. Instead, she looked back at the council room, where an occasional shout spilled into the hallway. "Shouldn't you be in that meeting? Or have you lost the king's favor?"

His face twitched, but before Lord Ewan could respond, a servant approached from behind him, clearing his throat and bowing slightly. "My lord, I've been looking all over for you. The king has granted your audience. He requests your presence in the council." The out of breath messenger indicated Lord Ewan move toward the room Morag had just left.

Lord Ewan raised a triumphant eyebrow, his gaze lingering on Morag for a moment longer before he turned away, leaving her with a parting sneer. "Do be careful, Morag. In these times of war, even palace fairies might find themselves expendable."

As he strode away, Morag balled her fists in a surge of frustration. She knew he was up to something, but until he acted overtly, there was little she could do. However, she ought to be more cautious, for the queen's sake and for the safety of the twins.

She shook off her ominous thoughts and continued her way through the darkening corridors, her senses heightened. In these halls, Morag had watched generations of kings and queens pass, each leaving their mark on the stone and tapestry of the kingdom. But now, the weight of the ongoing Kelpie Wars pressed heavily against the ancient walls, and she couldn't foresee what would come of it all.

Passing through the atrium, she spied a glint of metal at the end of a narrow cord hanging from a bronze candle sconce. *There you are.* She snatched the key and hung it back around her neck, relieved to have found it.

When she turned around, she almost collided with Solly.

"Och, Morag. Where did you get off to? Me and Mavis are going to the Queen's Garden to—" Solly had begun to make bouncing motions with her hands, which stopped as abruptly as her words. She reached out and touched the key. "I see you found it."

"Not now, Solly." Morag interrupted, waving her to go. Senna had gotten away from her, and she wanted to find her to see what she planned to do next. The lass was determined, but still young and in need of a fairy's guidance.

"Fine! I didnae want to tell you what I found digging in the garden, anyway." Solly turned and flew in the opposite direction, muttering under her breath. Servants paused to bow respectfully as she passed them, but she took no notice.

Morag was sorry to hurt Solly's sensitive feelings, but what was she to do? Her duty was to serve the ailing queen as best she could, even if that meant becoming increasingly preoccupied.

With the latest attacks, everyone, it seemed, had become increasingly preoccupied. The once-gleaming floors were clouded with dust. The passageways, lit with fewer candles, loomed as dreary as the dungeon. And it appeared as if the armory had spilled out into the main living quarters as soldiers kept their equipment at the ready.

As if attuned to her thoughts, warning bells rang out with urgency. *Clang. Clang. Clang.* A call to arms.

Immediately, doors along the hall opened and guards scrambled out. Morag flew out of their way and adjusted course for the main hall to find out what was happening.

As she arrived, a guard ran in through the open door. "They're coming out the river in droves, the devils."

Young soldiers, most of them still raw recruits being trained by Osario, raced past her, a blur of steel and determination. Female servants scurried about, fetching weapons and supplies, their faces drawn with resolve.

Amid the chaos, a booming voice cut through the air. "Stay strong, lads. You've prepared for this moment. We'll show them what Ainsley is made of." Osario emerged from the mass of soldiers, his imposing form standing out against the frenzied backdrop. If he saw her watching, this time he said nothing.

Spurred on by Osario's command, the soldiers stormed out of Ainsley Castle, their armor gleaming under the dull glow of torchlight. Their faces bore the weight of their responsibility to their kingdom.

As the thunderous departure of the soldiers faded, Morag found herself alone in the now-empty halls of the castle. A mantle clock in the next room went *tick, tick, tick,* as if this were an ordinary night.

Soon Solly, and then Mavis, joined her. Solly gave her a forgiving smile, her lips set in determination, and Morag returned the gesture. One of the best things about Solly was that she was quick to repair offenses.

"Seems like the kelpies noticed the level of the river going down," Morag said ominously. "Too bad."

"It had to happen sometime." Mavis clasped her hands. "Ready, then?"

The three nodded in agreement, then flew outside to do what they could to stop the latest invasion.

CHAPTER 4

KELPIES

The earthy scents of burning peat and blood assaulted the three fairies as much as the cold wind blowing down from the mountains. Torches and iron fire pots lit up the riverbank with a flickering orange light. As the trio flew across the lawn, the harsh wind, carrying particles of dust and small embers, fought against them.

In a kelpie war, instead of the clash of steel against steel, beastly roars and cries of pain rose above the battlefield. Kelpies used their size and speed to trample soldiers, and their teeth to shred their bodies. And if a kelpie managed to herd a man close to the water, there was little anyone could do to save themselves or others. The soldiers' main advantage was their weaponry, the kelpies' was their size and swiftness in their horse form.

"There," Mavis said, pointing downriver. "They've gone after the main bridge. I'll take the lead with Osario. Solly, come with me to run messages? And Morag?" Mavis glanced down at Morag's right side. "You hang back and guard the front door, aye?"

"Aye. I was going to volunteer for that job, anyway." Morag forced a smile.

Mavis gave her a sympathetic look before she and Solly set off to help.

The kelpies had attacked the main bridge before, but this time, they seemed to be getting somewhere. Already, several of the large stones closest to the water had been dislodged and looked ready to fall. Farther in, another group of kelpies attacked the center supports, attempting to collapse the bridge from the middle.

Kelpies hated the bridges that spanned the river. The stone bridges, especially, proved formidable. Large, sturdy structures, stone bridges impeded the kelpies' movement down the river and protected the townsfolk as they crossed from one side to the other.

Mavis was right to keep Morag close to the castle because of her weak side. She was a liability until she healed. Moving with care, Morag patrolled her area, senses alert to any sound or movement.

Calculating the time since Senna's dismissal, Morag figured the lass might have made it over the river before the attack, if she'd left immediately. If not, she'd still be on the castle grounds. Surely the lass wouldn't try to leave while the fighting was going on. That Morag even had the thought meant that it wasn't out of the realm of possibility.

Morag scanned the area, searching for any sign of Senna. The castle grounds seemed ominous under the moonlight, the shadows deep and concealing. However, none of the dark shapes looked like a young lass with packed bags sneaking away. Perhaps Senna had some sense, after all.

Oh, but there, upstream. Away from the lights, not Senna, but a lone kelpie rose onto the bank nearer to the stables.

Och, the sneak.

Of course, the stables might have been the kelpies' true objective all along. The bridge was merely a diversion.

But no kelpie was currently being held on the property. They'd learn that soon enough. Months ago, the king moved the kelpies that remained under his control and put them to work on his secret project upstream. But the kelpie prince, the true prize, had been moved separately to a location the king kept secret. Mavis had been trying to find it ever since, sneaking away at night, and flying as far away as she dared, convinced it must be hidden amongst the other kelpies in the heavily guarded area.

The winds soon caught the scent of the beast, a stench of rotten seaweed mixed with the metallic tinge of blood. It made Morag's stomach churn, but she swallowed down her revulsion. The blood did not come from the beast. Her keen eyes saw that it was unharmed.

Launching forward, she flew as fast as her damaged wing would allow. The sounds of the skirmish intensified near the river, but she pressed on toward the rogue kelpie until she caught its eye. The creature, large in comparison to her, stopped. It flicked its head, eyes gleaming as it focused on her. A low growl rumbled from its chest as it stomped its hoof, splattering mud in all directions.

"What you seek is not here," she said in a measured tone. "Go back whilst you still can." She pulled out her silver wand and stared the beast down. It knew what she was, where she came from, and who she represented. Would it dare challenge her?

It snorted in response, the sound like a sudden crash of waves against a rocky shore. The kelpie's nostrils flared as if seeking out what might be hidden in the stables. Disappointed, its eyes narrowed to dangerous slits. Its body tensed, muscles rippling as if getting ready to spring.

Undeterred, Morag stood her ground. She knew she could not physically stop the beast, but she could distract it. Cause it to doubt its course. Did it notice her mangled arm? The withered right wing, and her jerky flight?

With a sharp, guttural grunt, the kelpie lunged toward her, its powerful body propelled forward by long, lethal strides. Morag, unfazed by its terrifying display, braced herself.

No sooner had the kelpie lunged than a flash of steel hurtled past her, a javelin flung with deadly precision. It lodged into the kelpie's flank, eliciting an enraged roar from the creature. Soldiers of the royal guard burst onto the scene. Their voices bellowed orders, and their claymores glinted menacingly under the moonlight.

From across the distance, Mavis met Morag's gaze and nodded before focusing her attention back on the river.

While in horse form, an injured kelpie could retreat to the water, where it transformed back to water spirit and eventually healed. This is what made them so formidable. No matter how valiantly the soldiers fought, their efforts were only temporary, unless they could get the magical bridle off to prevent the transformation.

"Stop! Don't you touch her!" a young soldier commanded, standing firm in front of Morag, shielding her with his armored body. Morag gasped as she recognized the youth from dinner. The one who appeared so clumsy, clattering into the kitchen maid.

She sucked in her lips to hide a smile. She did love to see an act of chivalry and watch as a lad came into his own. She hovered temptingly near the kelpie as a distraction to the beast.

The kelpie reared on its hind legs, its dreadful shriek echoing throughout the castle grounds. More javelins flew as reinforcements arrived, keeping the creature at bay. Others worked to guide the kelpie away from the stables, maneuvering it toward an open field rather than back to the water where it could escape. In the field, they would pen it and get its bridle off so they could tame it.

After they moved away from her, Morag's adrenaline faded, and the pain in her injured arm and wing multiplied in stabbing pains. For relief, she dropped to the ground where she was at her most vulnerable. Fortunately, the king's guard had the situation under control and she retreated closer to the castle where she could watch in relative safety.

As she walked the path, a light in the queen's window drew her attention. Queen Cadha, her silhouette softly lit, stared out the window with a somber expression, watching the chaos unfold below. Her eyes, while distant, bore witness to the pandemonium beneath her. Her gaze fell on Morag, and a connection flickered in that moment.

Morag felt the weight of the queen's gaze upon her. She and Morag, the two of them damaged, yet pressing on. A kinship neither wanted.

The queen opened the window and held out her hand. As she did, a quiet rustling sound reached Morag's sensitive ears as a small bird flew straight for the opening and landed on the sill, something clutched in its beak.

The queen took it, then sent the bird off again. As the battle raged at the river, the queen nodded down at Morag, as if confirming that she'd allowed the palace fairy to witness the exchange.

"Aye, my queen. I see."

Morag's gaze returned to the battlefield where there was a shift in the action. Kelpies, though not defeated, were retreating for now. It was a never-ending battle for the citizens of Glenmoor Kingdom.

Solly and Mavis joined her, and they watched Osario lead the guards in caring for the injured men.

"They continue to toy with Glenmoor," Mavis said, her focus on the kelpies charging up and down the river.

Solly crossed her arms in frustration. "If only we could be rid of them. Force them back to the unseen world."

"Aye. Would that it were so easy," said Morag. "Until that day, we do what we can."

CHAPTER 5

OLD LENNOX

The morning after the attack, while the golden sun faithfully rose over the River Tarner, Queen Cadha lay in her bed, her frail body shrouded in a thick woolen blanket, despite the roaring wood fire in the fireplace. The room was hot in comparison to the usual peat fire, yet the queen still shivered.

A tepid bowl of water remained beside the bed with a bloated sponge sitting in the soapy water. Evidence that the queen didn't get out of bed this morning to see to her own needs. Each of her babies were tucked in beside her on top of the blanket, just the way she wanted them, their cherub-like mouths puckered in deep sleep.

Morag hovered near the window, waiting for the day nurse to finish her ministrations so Morag could talk to the queen privately. The nurse finished brushing the queen's hair for her and then took her sweet time plumping pillows and trying to talk the queen into sending the twins to the nursery.

"The wee things are fine...where they are," Cadha said, struggling for breath. "See...how well...they're sleeping?"

The day nurse looked at Morag as if to say: *Would you talk some sense?*

The queen shouldn't have kept watch last night. Today she could barely sit up properly, and her breathing labored between the words. Not two weeks back, Cadha had given birth to the twins. The prince and princess were tiny as tiny could be, but they were fighters and gained strength every day. And they were the sweetest bairns ever born as far as Morag was concerned.

The birth of the twins had brought a flicker of new hope to the kingdom. Two fresh souls, a reminder that the present leads to the future. But near the end of the pregnancy, the queen fell ill with a fever spike that'd left her frail, her lungs damaged. And her decline had only increased these last few days, leaving everyone at the castle concerned.

"Leave us, but send in Lennox, please," the queen instructed the nurse. "I—understand he's been waiting since before sunrise. I think he's waited long enough."

The nurse gathered the basin and sponge and gave a quick curtsy. "Your Majesty," she murmured, bowing slightly before slipping out, her expression etched with quiet concern.

Cadha turned to Morag. "I saw what you did last night, Morag. That took—real bravery."

"Och, away with ye." Morag brushed off the compliment but was well pleased.

"Good morn," interrupted Old Lennox as he hobbled into the room, a frail figure balancing an oversize leather bag filled with parchments, pens, and ink, along with his gnarled walking cane. Behind him one of the young attendants closed the door with a quiet click.

"You're looking as radiant as ever, my queen."

"Thank you, Lennox—you liar. Morag, we've more to discuss, so please stay," the queen said, her voice soft but firm.

"As you will." Morag retreated to the window, where she could keep an eye on the activities below and an ear to the discussion inside.

Near the bridge, soldiers scoured the battlefield for any injured that they had missed. Of the dead, nothing would be found, save their entrails left on the riverbank after the kelpies had drowned and consumed their victims. A terrible business all around.

A small pen near the stables contained two kelpies they'd caught in the battle, and nearby, the handful of men, bloody and bruised who had managed to take off the water horse bridles. Morag wondered what the king would do with those kelpies. It was dangerous to keep them on the property because the rest of the kelpies would continually be drawn to them. But it was also dangerous to move them, even though their magic bridles had already been removed and replaced with the royal silver ones that subdued them. To get them away from the castle, there had to be at least some water travel, which was always dangerous.

The stablemaster would likely work with them for a time before moving them to do the heavy work of reinforcing the bridges and banks along the Tarner. As long as they wore the king's bridles, they worked for the king.

Along the bank, rivermen fit new iron grates in the river, hammers clanging. Farther up to the west, Morag detected the rumble and splash of boulders crashing into the water. And to the east came the rhythmic pounding from rivermen driving wooden stakes into the riverbed, the sounds of a kingdom under siege. She turned her back on the frantic activity to focus on what mattered here in this room.

"And what of Senna?" the queen asked, her words carrying an air of authority despite her weakened state. It wasn't a casual question.

Senna! In all the excitement, Morag had forgotten to check on the lass.

Old Lennox sat on the plush chair near the foot of the bed and leaned his cane against the arm. He smiled, spreading his mustache across his lip. "Senna is like an alley cat. She always finds her feet. Do not worry, my queen. I hear she has found a place in town in the old mill." He looked warily at the door, as if wondering if it was safe to talk. "If she could stand before you, she would apologize for her recklessness."

Morag was relieved Senna made it across.

"Nonsense. When you next see her, send her...my gratitude. I'm proud of...her bravery to risk getting a worse...punishment than being exiled...from the castle." She looked at Old Lennox with fondness. "Now that...I have bairns of my own, my heart is both softer...and fiercer than I...expected. Folks don't know what...to make of me when I'm smiling and laughing one moment...and in tears the next. I can get away with much...these days as both a queen and a new mother."

"Shall I record that?" asked Lennox, attempting to inject some levity into the heavy conversation. He pulled a small worktable close and unloaded his parchment and writing implements.

"Och, Lennox," Queen Cadha sighed, a tender smile on her face as she looked at her sleeping children. "They have...filled my heart with a joy I never...knew possible. I completely understand your...tenderness...toward that rebel...girl of yours."

"All bairns have a little rebellion in them." He settled his reading glasses on his nose.

"They'll be one year old before we know it. Nine months...protected in my womb and already over ten days on their own. I wonder if I'll see their three months...for their naming ceremony to mark their first year of life." A wistful look overtook her, like she could turn back time to when they were still safe in her womb. She blinked, and the corners of her mouth lifted. "We'll need to agree...on their names for the...ceremony."

"I'm sure you and the king will come to an agreement by then."

"Aye. We must. And despite the darkness that surrounds our kingdom, I cannae help but hope for a brighter...future for all of us."

Old Lennox dipped his head, his quill poised over the parchment as he captured the queen's words. "Your Majesty, your children bring hope not only to you but to the entire kingdom. If we can stand strong against the kelpie invasion, they will grow up to lead our people well."

The queen nodded, her eyes glistening. "Aye, Lennox, that is my deepest desire. I look at them and am reminded that our lives have a greater purpose beyond our...numbered years. Tell me, honestly, before we continue, how fare...the children in our kingdom?"

Old Lennox hesitated, his eyes flicking to the floor for a moment. "Ye ken many of their parents have been lost in the fighting. There are too many orphans to tend. They are left vulnerable to the kelpies. Senna will be ready in a few days to move them out to the far villages where the attacks are fewer."

Queen Cadha's face grew somber. "It grieves me that our kingdom's children...are at risk. If only there was more we could do to protect them. The...best...course of action would be to end the fighting immediately."

"Aye," Old Lennox answered in such a tone as to attract Morag's attention. He was hiding something from the queen. That wasn't like Old Lennox.

Morag fluttered into his line of sight to give him a questioning look, but he refused to acknowledge her.

"Tell me what you have learned about the kelpies," said the queen. "What is it *specifically* that...they want? Not what my husband and the council have been telling...people."

"They want their prince released."

"What is the harm in letting their leader go? If we give them what they want, won't they leave us...alone? Or at least stop these constant assaults on our...kingdom? Why all the trouble now?"

Lennox glanced at Morag. As a fairy, Morag knew more about the kelpies than Lennox, but much of what she knew was not meant for human ears. They wouldn't believe it. And as the kingdom historian, Lennox also knew more about the kelpies than the people nowadays wanted to know. People preferred short memories to long historical records.

"Our kingdom has a long history of conflict with the kelpies.

They have no regard for human life, Cadha. If we give them what they want, they will take it all. Their prince will lead an attack that will destroy Glenmoor. Keeping him away from the rest of the kelpies is the only thing saving our kingdom."

Morag shifted. Lennox was both right and wrong. Yes, the kelpie prince wanted nothing more than to destroy the kingdom, and keeping the kelpies separated was a good strategy. But there was more than one way to save a kingdom.

"Is my husband going to relent and release their prince?"

"I cannae tell what is in your husband's mind. He is unpredictable."

"Aye, he is that." She smiled, a faraway look on her face. She blinked rapidly and came back to the moment. "A compromise. He could release the prince...but retain the magical bridle."

"He could." Lennox waited, the look of a patient teacher on his face.

"But they won't just want the prince, will they? They'll never leave until they...get his bridle back, too, so that he can transform into a water...spirit again. What else is in your archives, Lennox? There must be some knowledge...about the kelpies that can help...us now."

"Morag might have more to speak on that." He looked pointedly in her direction.

Morag glared at Lennox. There were some things about the unseen world she was not willing to share. "I only ken we don't give in. The king could move the prince and the bridle away from any rivers, but as long as there is water, or underground springs, the kelpies can travel and will find them there."

"He will never agree to some...remote location. He insists on keeping all...his treasures at hand." Cadha glanced at Lennox. "At least, as many as he can, given the circumstances."

"Aye." Lennox studied the queen's expression.

She was a woman with nothing to lose and everything to gain for her children. She had days, maybe weeks, left to live. A month if she would stay in bed and rest. Let others, like herself, care for the kingdom's heirs.

"Lennox," Queen Cadha began, her voice soft and measured. "I worry about you as well. Your...relationship with the king...it is not as it should be."

Old Lennox gave a quiet sigh, his eyes momentarily distant. "Aye, Your Majesty. The king and I...our views often differ."

Morag could see the worry etched on the old man's face. He was afraid—not for himself, but most likely for his daughter, for the kingdom. Morag had always admired Lennox's dedication to his work, even though his relationship with the king was tenuous at best.

He continued. "I worry, Queen Cadha," Lennox confessed, his voice low, "In the current circumstances, I ought to take extraordinary steps to preserve our archives."

"You have no trust in our soldiers?" Cadha sounded disappointed.

"I willnae wait to see how it plays out either way. The knowledge I have must be protected for your bairns when they need it. I've shared copies of the most pertinent documents with the king, but he was dismissive. So, if you don't mind my candor, I'd like to take precautions."

Queen Cadha gave a nod even while her fingers twisted her signet ring. A nervous habit whenever she was working a problem.

Suddenly, the heavy wooden door of the queen's chamber swung open. King Seamus strode in, his bushy eyebrows furrowed over his piercing gaze. With a full beard and stout stature, he was an imposing figure, even when he wasn't trying to be. From the adjoining sitting room, Morag heard the clatter of dropped silver, quickly silenced, as the queen's attendants fumbled their tasks. Immediately, Morag flitted as far into the shadows as she could.

Lennox and Queen Cadha straightened; their conversation halted. The air thickened as the king looked from the queen to Lennox, a stormy expression shading his face.

"I did not expect to find you here, Lennox," the king said.

"Your Majesty," Lennox replied, holding up a parchment. "I was recording the queen's words for the annals of our kingdom." His defiance was subtle, but Morag could sense it.

Seamus grunted. "I can provide you with testimony later. As you can see, the queen is not well and needs her rest."

"My heart, thank you for your concern, but I'm right enough to make the record. Our children will want to read about their early days...along with the heroic exploits of their father," Queen Cadha added, her gaze steady on the king and her breath careful. There was a challenge in her voice alongside the compliment, a reminder that she, too, had a right to mark the history of their kingdom.

Morag watched, her breath held, as the king nodded tersely, his eyes never leaving Lennox.

Lennox began to gather his supplies, quickly wiping off the nib of his pen and tucking it carefully into a pocket in his satchel. "We've had a long enough session, my queen. I'll take my leave while you rest. I can bring in the documents for you to read later." Lennox bowed to the king. "My king." Then he looked at Morag through his lashes while he shuffled out. His expression conveyed that he needed to talk to her.

CHAPTER 6
MORAG'S MISSION

As Lennox disappeared into the adjoining sitting room, Morag wished she had been alert enough to follow him. Now, she dared not move and attract the king's notice. The king and queen were used to servants all around them, but the king had developed a dislike for the palace fairies and a particular dislike for Morag.

"Would you like to hold the bairns?" the queen asked her husband. "They've been fed and willnae wake if you pick them up."

Seamus paled and shook his head. "I don't want to risk it."

"Risk? That's an interesting choice of word for your flesh and blood." Cadha pinned him with her gaze. "I hope you won't risk your bairns...for anything."

The king patted his chest, glancing around the room as if looking for escape. He mumbled something about a council meeting and then backed out the door.

Morag quietly let out a breath, glad that the exchange was over and she managed to stay out of it. As far as she knew, the king had yet to hold his heirs.

Queen Cadha's gaze stared at the thick wooden door. "Did...you see...the way...he looked at them? His own flesh and blood and yet he keeps his distance." She eased the control she had over her breathing while the king was in the room, and her eyes welled with tears.

"Perhaps it's nerves," Morag offered. "They are quite wee, and he's at war with the kelpies." Morag didn't understand the king's hesitation either, not for certain, anyway.

Cadha didn't look like she'd been comforted. Quite the opposite. As her brows furrowed deeper, she deflated, folding up inside herself now that the king was no longer in the room. "Morag, are you able to sneak out of the palace and get word to Senna?"

"I cannae fly across the Tarner, if that's what you're asking." Morag was ashamed to remind the queen of her failings. There was a time when Morag could fly for hours, soaring with the eagles without getting tired or a muscle cramp in her wing.

The queen nodded. "I...was...hoping to find other...means." Her breathing was beginning to take visible effort. "Across one of...the bridges, possibly...hidden...in a cart?"

No one was to leave the palace without Osario's or the king's permission, a restriction that could lead to desperate measures, as seen recently with the lengths Senna was willing to go to in order to get to town, all with the queen's approval and blessing.

"With help from Mavis or Solly, perhaps." One of them could cause a disturbance like the kelpies did at the main bridge, and she could climb into a crate.

"Nae..." There was a long pause as the queen tried to find her breath. "You...alone. I want to know if it is possible...to slip...through the castle's defenses with...no one knowing. No one else...helping."

Morag imagined her path. She'd have to hide in something being transported into town. A container of sorts that could avoid detection at the checkpoints. She rose to her full height. "What message shall I bring?"

"Tell Senna...to be ready...to go...at my signal."

"Which is?"

The corners of the queen's lips fell, and her chest sank in with a deep exhale. "When me bairns are...safely...deposited on...her doorstep."

Morag stared at the queen, not quite believing her ears. "Nae, my queen. I thought we were only making plans for the orphan children to leave town." Morag's voice was laced with confusion, her brows furrowing as she tried to grasp the gravity of the queen's words. "Senna is safely off. Why add more complexity to her task?" And with the palace fairies to guard the royal offspring, they were safest at the castle.

The queen, her eyes weary yet determined, met Morag's gaze steadily, one hand resting gently on the slumbering form of the little prince nestled beside her. "Don't look at me...like I'm making...a...bad...decision. I'm aware...of the state...of our kingdom." Again, she paused to catch her breath. "And the state of my husband. To leave...them here...after I'm gone...is to remove...their...greatest...protection." She paused for breath after her impassioned speech, her fingers trailing softly over the prince's downy hair.

If Morag could heal the queen, she would. But as it was, she couldn't even ease her suffering. Morag's own arm throbbed, a reminder that the fairies were vulnerable here, too. She couldn't honestly tell the queen otherwise.

"I need to know...they are safe, Morag. I know you...and the others...will do all you can, but you have to admit..." The long pause hurt Morag's heart as her queen struggled again. "The best course would be for them to leave." The queen's gaze drifted toward the window, where the first light of dawn shone through with a steady light. "The kelpies are getting too brazen, and if the king...won't even hold his own bairns..." Her voice trailed off, leaving the worry hanging in the air.

The little princess, sensing the shift in her mother's mood, stirred and let out a small whimper. After a few strokes of a mother's loving hand, she soon settled back into sleep.

The queen was too observant and correct, as usual. Morag discretely massaged her damaged arm, trying to relax the knotted muscle. "Aye," Morag agreed. "I've noticed his aloofness goes beyond the nerves of being a new father."

"Some have suggested we offer...a...sacrifice like other kingdoms do...when they have a dragon problem. Are you...aware?" Cadha bent over and kissed the princess's head.

"Aye." Morag had hoped to spare Cadha the moral downfall of her kingdom. Someone else—likely Lennox—had filled in the gaps Morag had left out.

"Are we that...desperate, Morag? Or have we...lost our way?"

"The kelpies have been brutal. You see how young some of the new guards are? But, yes, I fear sentiments continue to shift, and we are in trouble."

"My mother used to tell me stories about the magic you fairies would do in our kingdom. How...Solly would go around town waving up flowers, so the town was always...beautiful and fragrant. Mavis...somehow...had the effect of keeping the streets...tidy and the lads from getting into fights. And for you, my mother...said you...would provide wishing wells and guiding lights at night. Fun things...that made our land...special. I've never seen you do any of that. Why don't you anymore?"

Morag chuckled. "Solly helped with some of those." She sighed, remembering those times. "The kingdom has changed. Hearts have hardened, and that hinders what we can do."

Cadha nodded. "I think...my heart was hard...for a time, but it grows...softer by the day." She kissed the wee prince. "'Tis only a matter of time...before interest turns toward...me bairns, Morag. They'll say...it's a proper lesson...to the people that even the king won't...spare his own for the good of the kingdom. To set...an example for when their children...are demanded next."

Morag had no words. The conversation she'd overheard at dinner wasn't the first time she'd heard the proposal. And now the queen had reached the logical conclusion, as horrific as it was. What could be done for a kingdom whose people sacrificed their children for the supposed good?

Queen Cadha met Morag's gaze, her expression grave. "I want

me bairns away from here so they have...a chance to live. So no one can...hold them...hostage, be he kelpie or king. I want that...for all the orphans who will have no one...to fight for them." She paused, her gaze intensifying. "All will know...soon enough, but for now, we must keep talk like this between us. Not even Old Lennox can know."

Morag nodded, though her heart was heavy. The king had grown more unpredictable as the war progressed, his decisions increasingly fraught with danger. "There must be some other—"

"This is the only way I'll feel secure enough...in their future...so that I may go with any...peace." The queen's gasping voice cracked with emotion. "Morag? Don't deny me this." Her eyes, once bright, were now dulled by sorrow.

"Then let me bring the other palace fairies in to help." Morag cradled her bad arm for emphasis in case the queen had forgotten her limitations. "They will know I'm up to something. A secret won't bother Mavis, but Solly could get annoyed, and overly curious."

The queen managed a rueful smile, a faint spark of her former self flickering in her eyes. "I need you all...acting normally. The fewer who know about...my plans, the better." She reached out, her hand resting briefly on Morag's. "It's not because...I don't trust them, and you have my permission to make...quick decisions and change plans if you see a...better way. But no matter what you do, Morag, promise me that me bairns will grow up...safely away from...all this until the Kelpie Wars...have ended."

Morag's voice caught in her throat as she answered. "Aye, Cadha. The bairns have always had my allegiance. I will do what I can. However, I can only promise actions, not outcome. The results are not in my control." Her words were a solemn vow, a promise that she intended to keep.

"Thank you, Morag. That's enough...for me. Now, go and find...an escape route for these precious souls."

CHAPTER 7

BEING WATCHED

Morag's path took her to a side entrance of the castle where the household staff bustled with their daily task of unloading supply carts. Beyond them, the River Tarner, a natural barrier as formidable as any wall, seemed to mock her with its swirling currents and hidden enemies. There was the main stone bridge over the river, as well as several smaller bridges that crossed the canals which formed a moat around the castle. Guards stood at attention at both ends of the bridges, and there was a scout in the middle watching the water.

Morag didn't like her chances. Not at all. *But I'm about the queen's business and will complete my task with excellence.*

She carefully watched the staff, who worked with baskets and crates. Goods such as foodstuffs and repaired weapons returned, while broken weapons and laundry went out.

The head laundress, a plump and jovial woman with an ear for gossip, took time to motivate her crew. "Step it up, lasses," she called to the line of younger women, each carrying heavy woven baskets overflowing with linen sheets. "We'll not get it all done at this rate."

Morag had never quite considered how or when the laundry left the castle. "Excuse me," Morag called out, her voice carrying just a hint of curiosity as she approached. "Might I ask where you're taking the castle's laundry?"

The laundress glanced up before dropping the basket into a cart beside several others. "It's to the washerwomen in town. We've small facilities here for the royals' bits and bobs themselves, but for the rest of us, we send it out. Besides, he don't want us risking going down to the river at present, do he? He'd rather the town women get eaten by kelpies than us." The laundress didn't look too bothered by her own words.

Morag raised her eyebrows before nodding thoughtfully. Her eyes flicked to the wooden cart pulled by donkeys. "And how often does the laundry leave the castle?"

"Twice a week, on Wednesdays and Saturdays," the laundress replied, wiping her hands on her apron. "Why do ye ask, dear?"

"Just curious," Morag said, her mind working quickly. She studied the cart's construction, noting the organization of the baskets heaped inside. There was just enough space for her, she reckoned, if she curled up nice and small.

The laundress tapped the side of the cart. "That's all for today. Ta-ra."

The hostler clicked his tongue to get the donkey moving, and the cart rocked and groaned as it moved forward.

Morag followed behind to observe how the guards reacted when the cart reached the bridge.

Positioning herself near the bank of the Tarner, Morag rested under the protection of a beech tree, whose leaves were beginning to turn a lovely golden bronze. From there, she observed the traffic on the bridge and watched how the guards decided who to allow across.

There were three carts lined up at the bridge before the laundry cart joined them. The guards thoroughly searched all of them. When it came to the laundry, they merely jabbed a blunt pole into each bundle. Morag winced with each jab, imagining how it would feel to be poked in such a way. *Too risky.*

In fact, the guards were so good at their jobs—lifting tarps, climbing on board to get to crates packed high, making a woman take off her coat and going through her pockets—that Morag knew she'd seen enough. If the king was that paranoid about what was exiting the castle grounds, there was no way she'd be able to sneak the babies through by the road.

In Morag's opinion, Mavis and Solly ought to spirit the twins away under cover of darkness, but the queen specifically stated that only Morag could be involved. Until she could convince the queen otherwise, she would operate under the queen's guidance and look for another way.

How else can I secret the bairns away without help from anyone else?

A boat might not be as carefully searched, given how no one liked to be out on the water for longer than necessary. But that had risks of its own. Morag couldn't let the babies get so close to the water because of the danger of the lurking kelpies. Last night and this morning's cleanup were stark reminders of that.

Och, I can barely see a thing from down on the ground. Morag eyed the distance to the far bank, wondering when she had last flown that far. At the castle, there were many perches she could land on and rest before continuing on. Her wings were not as capable since the king damaged her right side, and, regretfully, she'd not pushed herself much to improve her lot.

She moved to the edge of the bank and peered down. The Tarner flowed deceptively slowly along the surface, carrying the odd fallen log and branches—the work of the men upriver trying to clog the flow. "None of you nasty beasts down there?" she whispered.

The cool, silver-streaked water shimmered gently in the midmorning light. Often, the morning mist on a cold day hovered and swirled above the river, making it seem like kelpies were about, even if they weren't. River kelpies could manipulate the water to help them rise up, so it was always wise to be wary around the water, no matter how calm.

Not seeing anything untoward in the water, Morag leaped

into the air. She climbed higher and higher, wondering when she would top out. It would take boldness to help the kingdom get out of the mess it was in. And Morag could rise to the occasion in more ways than one. However, halfway across the Tarner, she realized that she was descending. Slowly at first, and then rapidly. She just didn't have the strength, as she'd feared.

The swirling surface of the river was coming at her fast and then her toes grazed the water. A jolt of adrenaline shot through her. She pumped her wings harder, sending her upward again. She winced as pain knifed through her right side. "Och, I'm rusty," she muttered. "It's been too long." She veered closer to the bridge. If need be, she'd land and face the condescension of the guards and questions from Osario.

Morag's heart skipped a beat as she dropped closer to the water, as if being pulled in. She looked closer and her heart skipped again as an unblinking eye watched her from under the surface. She should have noticed him from a greater distance. Were her eyes beginning to fail her, too? She scowled at the beast and pulled herself up, away from harm's way.

A shout came from the riverbank. "Hey! The king says the palace fairies are to stay on castle grounds."

Annoyed at being caught unawares by the kelpie and now by a palace guard, Morag berated herself. She'd just proven how hard it would be to sneak herself away, let alone two infants who, while they were good sleepers, were, as the nanny noted, known to have a good set of lungs on them. Especially the princess.

With indignation toward the guard, she said—in her best imitation of Solly—"You've got a kelpie here, you know." She pointed to the location in the river and was pleased when the guard scrambled to the middle of the bridge to see for himself.

She fluttered awkwardly back to the castle side of the Tarner to report what she'd learned to the queen.

CHAPTER 8
WHAT ABOUT DARIA?

Morag returned to the queen's chambers, softly closing the heavy door behind her. Queen Cadha lay propped up in bed, the thick wool blanket drawn up to her chest, her eyes closed.

The heavy curtains entombed the room in near darkness, with only the flickering glow from embers in the fireplace dancing eerily across the queen's features, casting shadows that aged her. The babies were asleep in the cradle at the foot of the bed, hidden behind veils.

Taking the same chair that Lennox had used, Morag sat to wait for the queen. They could both get some rest before they attempted to tip the balance in the twins' favor.

"I'm awake, Morag." The queen's eyes stayed closed.

"How did ye ken it were me?"

"You always smell like...heather...from the moors. Extra damp heather...at the...moment. What happened?"

"It's impossible, my queen. Even if the bairns were as quiet and still as the unmovable mountains, we wouldn't make it across. Everything is searched. Even the river, though I wouldn't chance a crossing with your bairns, anyway. There's a kelpie out there now, lying low under the surface." Morag's voice was laced with frustration as she paced to the window and parted the curtains to look out at the sparkling river.

"Nothing is...impossible, Morag. You've told me that...time and again."

Morag turned back to the oppressive room. She longed to throw open the curtains and banish the darkness, but the queen's eyes were so sensitive to strong daylight. Even the flickering candle at her bedside might be too bright. Morag fumbled inside her pocket, looking for her snuffer. *Och, where's the thing when you need it?*

"Have ye lost...something again, Morag?"

"Nae," she said, patting her pockets absently. "It'll turn up." Only another trivial object. Her snuffer for the candles she helped put out at night. She licked her fingers before pinching the flame.

Cadha's lips were set like she wasn't surprised at Morag's poor report. Her hands, resting on the blanket, clenched slightly in a gesture of frustration. "You saw me receive...a note last night?"

"Aye." Morag walked away from the window, her gaze meeting the queen's.

Queen Cadha shifted in her bed, wincing slightly from the effort. She pushed herself up a little higher against the plush pillows, her eyes reflecting the firelight. "There's...a woman. A traveler. She never stays...in one place too long, but she sends me...messages."

"The bird."

"Aye. And the...mysterious bard seen in town. This time, she sent...a poem. A bit...curious, and I wonder if it might...help us. She has...the most amazing timing." The queen's voice held a hint of wonder, mixed with hope.

"Show me." Morag perched on the edge of the bed, her attention fully on Cadha.

"I memorized it before...burning the parchment." The queen recited softly:

"In fields where leaps the timid hare,
trust burrowed paths to solve despair."

She spread her hands helplessly, her brow furrowed in thought. "What...do you think? Does she want us to...consult with the hares? Do you...have the gift?"

"Nae, animals don't communicate with me, at least not in ways I easily understand. Nor Mavis or Solly, though Solly likes to pretend they do." Morag glanced at the unicorn tapestry hanging on the wall, its vibrant colors muted in the firelight. A keen eye would see the plethora of animals stitched behind the regal figure, but because the threads were so dark, they blended seamlessly, all but disappearing in comparison. "You think the hares might have a way out?"

The queen frowned. "Not that I...completely understand the message either, but now that I know...what I have to do, the poem makes...more sense. At first, I thought...they would give me another method...of sending messages, that maybe...someone had noticed the birds. Now I am hopeful that she means to...help us find a way out for me bairns."

"Burrowed paths...the rabbits burrow, but do hares?" Morag wrinkled her nose. "I don't think they do."

"You fairies have taught me...to look for the unexpected; that's oft where...the answers are found," Cadha said, her voice carrying a note of wisdom gained from years of ruling a kingdom embroiled in magic and danger. "There are always unseen forces at work," Morag agreed. She let her gaze drift toward the window where the gentle rustling of leaves served as a reminder of the world outside Ainsley's stone walls. She thought for a moment. She remembered Solly's eagerness to talk about the garden, and her complaints about holes. Also, Solly'd been making bouncing motions, like a hare would make. Morag smiled. With rising enthusiasm, she said, "And forces are never more so at work than in the queen's own garden. I suspect we've been overrun with hares as of late. I'll go find out."

Cadha slid to the edge of the bed. "I want to go, too. I'll...take the bairns for some air and help you...discover the true meaning of the poem." Her voice held a trace of longing as she swung her legs over the edge of the bed, her feet touching the cold stone floor. She attempted to stand, but her strength betrayed her, and she swayed unsteadily. Morag was at her side in an instant, her arms offering support, steadying the frail queen.

"Let me go on an expedition first. There is no need you exerting yourself for nothing." Morag's tone was gentle yet firm. The queen would pay for this sudden burst of adrenaline if she didn't go back to bed.

Cadha's eyes shimmered, the firelight reflecting in them. "'Tis not for...nothing. Me bairns have barely seen...the sky. Cooped up...with me...in this room because I can't bear to be...without them for long. I've been a...shameful mother not...introducing them to their land." Her voice cracked with emotion, her gaze falling to the thick plush rug at her feet. "I know it's near time...for me to...let go, but before I do, I want to do...proper activities with them. See as many of their firsts as I can. They would enjoy...the garden, aye?"

Cadha, her energy waning, sank back into the pillows, her face growing deathly pale against the rich evergreen bed linens. Morag patted the young queen's hand comfortingly, her own heart heavy. The queen was talking nonsense, but there would be no reasoning with her now.

"I'll go to the garden to see what I can see. You rest up for those sweet bairns and I'll report back."

"Wait, Morag." Cadha's voice was faint, but there was a hint of urgency in it. "Do any...humans at the castle have...the gift? There must be someone."

The queen sounded desperate for the first time, and it broke Morag's heart to hear it so. Morag hesitated, her intuition wrestling with her doubts. "Aye, perhaps the kitchen maid named Daria, though if she does, she barely knows it yet."

"Then take...the maid. But only tell her...what is necessary...for her help; don't tell her any more just yet. We need...to test her to see if she'll be up...to the task. If we need her to take the bairns when the time...comes." The queen began to cough.

"You would trust Daria to take the bairns? I thought—I assumed you were asking me. Or even one of your loyal nurse-maids would make more sense? Even that overprotective nanny?" Morag couldn't hide the disappointment beneath her words. She loved those bairns. Pledged to watch over them. Perhaps the queen worried that Morag would lose the children like she'd lost so many other things lately?

The queen's cough continued, tears streaming down her red face as her body convulsed while her lungs fought for air.

The door burst open, and the day nurse rushed in to aid the queen, supporting the Cadha's shoulders and speaking calm but firm words. "Easy breaths, Your Majesty, easy now." The nurse poured water into a cup and waited for a break in the fit. Her sharp look at Morag suggested the palace fairy should have already been holding the cup at the ready.

Several attendants from the other room also crowded into the doorway. One clutched a spare linen, another bit her lip, all eyes fixed on the struggling queen. Morag wanted to tell them it wasn't Cadha's time yet, but she remained quiet. They all wanted to help, and if standing in the doorway gawking made them feel better, she'd let them stand there.

Finally, there was a pause, and the queen reached out a shaking hand. She gulped water between coughs until her breathing steadied. Reassured, some of the attendants returned to their duties.

Meanwhile, the babies woke up, startled by the commotion.

The nanny rushed in next, cinching the pale sash at her waist as if preparing for battle. Her sharp eyes took in the scene—the gasping queen, the attending nurse—before she turned decisively to the cradle. She scooped the two up in an instant. "'Tis time for their baths, anyway. I'll take them now." She was out the door before the queen could protest, even if she wanted to. Cadha looked sadly at the door where her babies had disappeared.

"Thank you," she said to the remaining nursemaid. "That is all."

The day nurse reluctantly left, shoving the water pitcher into Morag's hands first. Morag's eyes softened, tears welling up. "Thank you," she said meaningfully to the nurse. "I'll be quicker next time." She said it even though there was nothing she could have done until the queen's fit had ended.

The nursemaid nodded tersely. She shuffled the remaining attendants out of her way and then closed the door behind all of them.

"I should go, too," Morag said. "Is there anything else?"

Cadha smoothed her expression, though her eyes remained bloodshot. "The bairns would be more...comfortable with their nanny...but she's only ever lived at the castle...her mother served the previous queen. Nae, and at her age on the run...living off...the moors or in a forest...hideaway?" The queen shook her head firmly. "I need someone young. Someone with...gumption. Senna...obviously is capable, and I suspect...Daria is, too."

"Aye," Morag agreed.

Morag stood to leave when the queen reached out and grasped her hand, her grip surprisingly strong.

"I have...another job for you, when...the time is right, Morag." Cadha's voice was soft but filled with conviction. "Something that...only you can do."

CHAPTER 9
THE PATH

Troubled by the queen's growing desperation, Morag hurried to the kitchen to look for Daria. What job would the queen have for her other than protecting the twins?

Enticing aromas of garlic, thyme, and freshly baked bread wafted through the air as if everything were normal in the castle.

As if they weren't under siege in a way they'd never been before.

As if the futures of the wee prince and princess weren't being crafted and twisted behind the scenes.

Morag hovered high in the kitchen rafters, trying to be as unobtrusive as possible. Now and then, a scullery maid would glance up, squinting at the fairy, before returning to her task. The kitchen maids seemed not to notice her at all, their attention focused on peeling and chopping at the long wooden tables laden with potatoes, carrots, and parsnips, while the cook shouted instructions at them and stirred onions in sizzling pans.

Not seeing Daria anywhere, Morag approached a young maid, who was vigorously scrubbing a pot with several more piled up beside her. Morag knew the girl and Daria were friendly. "Excuse me," Morag said, raising her voice to be heard over the din, "have you seen Daria?"

The girl pointed toward the gardens without looking up. "Gone to gather herbs for dinner, she has. You might find her at the far side of the garden."

Morag nodded, mouthing a soft "thank you" before making her way to the outside exit, only to run into Osario at the door, arms crossed.

"No need to guard the supplies when the kitchen is full of staff, is there?" she asked, making her distaste regarding how he'd handled the Senna situation earlier obvious to everyone there.

"Maybe I've got my eye on you," he said, his voice rough.

Morag didn't know how to respond, so she shrugged and pushed her way through the door and out into the kitchen garden. Osario followed her outside but exited the garden toward the field by the barracks.

Morag had heard that in Osario's youth he was a jokester. But ever since she'd known him, he wore a rigid mask that made everyone around him stick to the task at hand. Joking or not, he was a formidable foe to anyone who got in his way.

In contrast to the busy kitchen, the garden was a picturesque scene. Bees meandered from flower to flower, bathed in sunlight. The late-summer garden was winding down its production, with very few tomatoes left on the vine. Rows of cabbages and carrots and leeks grew in orderly plots and tall trellises supported a variety of growing squashes. Somewhere between the plots and hidden by the trellises, a maid was singing. Following the tune, Morag found Daria snipping parsley into her basket.

Daria's brown hair was tied up in a messy bun, loose strands framing her freckled face. Her worn apron was covered in dirt smudges, and her cheeks were rosy from the sun. As she worked, a couple of birds flitted about her, singing in rhythm with her song.

"There you are lass. I need you to come with me." Morag didn't wait for a reaction, she simply expected Daria to obey a palace fairy and follow.

Daria quickly wiped her hands on her apron and bent to pick up the woven grass basket at her feet. "Where are we going?"

Without answering, Morag headed toward a more secluded part of the garden, behind the bean poles and away from prying eyes. Once there, she asked, "Do ye ken you can speak to the animals in a way that's special?"

"What do you mean?"

"The birds just now. They were singing with you."

Daria laughed. "Nae, I was singing with them. I do it all the time."

Morag raised a brow in curiosity. "Do ye now?"

"Aye, my mother, God bless her, taught me how. Tis easy, so say the women in my family. It's all a matter of paying attention and then joining in."

Just what Morag wanted to hear. She waved Daria out of the kitchen garden and down a path that would take them to the Queen's Garden. "Have you been able to teach any of the other maids to sing with the birds?"

Daria shook her head. "They've not the patience. They all tell me I'm away with the fairies when I do it." She cast a sidelong glance at Morag, regret evident in her eyes. "I'm sorry to use the expression in your presence. I mean nothing by it." She shifted her basket. "In fact, I prefer to be away with the fairies, ye ken?"

Morag touched Daria's arm. "I ken. Perhaps it's a gift you have. A talent to be used when a palace fairy comes round and asks for help?" Morag raised her eyebrows meaningfully.

Daria hesitated, her grip tightening on her basket. "Is this what's going on? You want me to sing with the birds?"

Morag leaned in closer, her voice barely above a whisper. "Not the birds. Have you called to any other animals?"

Daria paused, memories flitting across her face. "Perhaps I have. I've gotten up right close to some: a red squirrel, a pine martin, but mostly birds, even a funny capercaillie once. I find thems with wings easiest to get on with."

"A pine martin? *Hmm.* That's promising. Do you feel like you know what they're communicating to you? Almost as if they were speaking to you?" She tugged Daria forward, pulling her toward the hedge bordering the Queen's Garden.

"Like a conversation? No, not in words."

"In feeling? An intuition that you know their meaning?"

Daria's gaze dropped to the ground as she thought. "I've not considered it much before. Not in words, no. But feelings, maybe." She met Morag's gaze. "You've given me something to think on."

Morag, sensing the lass's unease, offered a comforting smile. "It's a rare gift, Daria. One that might prove invaluable. Are ye willing to give it a go for me? Stretch yourself and see what gift you've been given?" They were at the entrance to the Queen's Garden now, and Morag stopped.

Osario's voice echoed up from the field where he was training the recruits, and Daria looked their way, even though they couldn't be seen from here. Morag recalled the young guard who'd made the lass blush yesterday. *Aye, the lass knows secrets.* But where would her loyalty lie when the time came?

"Have a think right here," Morag said, knowing that Solly would have too many questions if she saw Morag bring Daria round. "I'll pop into the garden first to make sure that we are alone."

Morag took to the air, the most efficient way to see where everyone was. There was Daria, straining to see where the guards were going through their paces. Past a row of trees and in the field, Osario had them lined up in battle stance, oblivious to the curious maid not far away.

The familiar ache formed on her right side as Morag rose too high. She renewed her focus and flew over the hedge and into her beloved queen's garden.

The Queen's Garden was an outdoor refuge on the edge of Ainsley Castle. Lush roses grew beside lavender and alyssum. The late summer sun that warmed the petals and the air alike brought a comfortable heat to her skin, along with the sweet floral scent.

Aye, the queen and the bairns would be revived here if Cadha could muster the strength.

Morag flew round the trees, simultaneously looking for anyone in the garden—Solly in particular—and also looking for signs of hares waiting to assist the queen.

In the center of the garden, a fountain topped with a weathered unicorn statue gushed water in an arc from the unicorn's horn. The droplets caught the sunlight and cast tiny rainbows. The horn's once-sharp point was worn smooth by decades of running water.

Solly knelt nearby in a bed of wilted plants, furtively touching each one and reviving it, her attempts to extend the summer growing season. When she saw Morag, she stood and tried to get her attention by waving her wide-brimmed gardening hat.

"Mavis wants to speak with you!"

"I'll see her later. Thank you." Morag continued her sweep of the garden, but Solly rose to the air and followed after her.

"What are you looking for?"

"You started to tell me about holes in the garden, so I thought I'd see for myself."

"Holes? Aye, troublesome things. Almost as troublesome as palace fairies asking sideways questions. What's really on your mind, Morag?"

"Your troublesome holes are on my mind! No need to read into everything I do."

"I've taken care of them already, but by tomorrow they'll be back if you want to come by and see them then." She flew in front of Morag. "You're not planning to cross the river alone, are you?" she chastised. "I saw you earlier. What were you thinking, trying such a thing in daylight? The king has strict orders for us to stay on this side of the river."

"Hush. Are you trying to get me in trouble with the king?"

"You weren't in the dining hall this morning," Solly accused.

"Nae, I had other things to do."

Solly tilted her curly head. "Besides eat? What things? I know everything you do and you don't have *things* to do at breakfast time."

Satisfied the rest of the garden was empty, Morag circled back and dropped down beside the fountain. She practically tasted the garden's tang, the rich earth and freshness of growing things. *Now, how to move Marisol along?*

"What does Mavis want? Could you help her?"

Solly crossed her arms and huffed. "She wouldn't tell me." She leaned forward and narrowed her eyes. "Are you two keeping secrets?"

"I haven't seen Mavis since last night. I've been busy elsewhere of late."

Aside from the queen's request for secrecy, Morag really didn't want to tell Solly because the news would find its way to the far corners of the castle. Solly wasn't good with secrets.

"Och, it's those bairns, isn't it? They've got most of the female-kind all fighting for a glimpse, making excuses to run errands to the queen's chambers."

Morag let out a sigh of relief. This she could answer honestly. "They are bonny, Solly. Have you seen 'em? I'd do anything to make sure they grow up healthy and happy."

"Barely got a peek in yet." Solly looked affronted. "That nanny keeps turning me away. Says I'm too much for the queen and bairns right now. Too much! Whatever does she mean by that? They'll be a-walkin' before I get my time."

"You should go see them now," Morag said and gave her a slight push. It didn't take much to send Solly on a path of mischief. "They've been taken out for a bath, so you'll not be turned away at the nursery, like you might at the queen's door. And even so, you could send the overprotective nanny away with a big enough *nudge* that you can slip in and see the bairns undisturbed."

Solly looked wary. "Are you encouraging a frivolous nudge?" Then she lit up. "Oh, aye. I'll bring them flowers—their first. What shall they be? Primroses or harebells?" She clapped her hands. "Why not both?" She snipped several choice cuttings before flying away. "Thanks, Morag!"

Relieved to be alone in the garden, Morag retrieved Daria. "Just us," Morag said. She led the way in through the gardener's gate, still searching in vain for any place a hare could hide. She'd seen no evidence of hares, nor of any holes Solly had missed covering up.

"Och, it's bonny in here," Daria said, her eyes wide. "Never been in before." She danced her fingers over an exceptionally large primrose and leaned in for a smell.

"I need you to call out the hares."

Daria snatched her hand back, as if reminded she was there for a purpose. "I'll try." She looked lost for a moment, then held up her hands helplessly. "I usually have a task at hand and the words flow from that. Is there any work I can do?"

Morag looked around, at a loss. The garden was pristine, carefully manicured and maintained for any moment the queen might want to return to it. "Solly won't mind if you do some weeding. There are always weeds in a garden, aren't there?"

Daria grinned. "I'll check." She settled under a golden sycamore, and as she parted green sections of bog myrtle, she began to sing, making up words as she worked. Spinning a tale of a palace fairy who needed the help of the castle hares.

Soon, there was a rustle in the hedge near the river side of the garden. A small group of three hares emerged, their brown ears perked and dark eyes fixed on Daria. She faltered for just a moment, sending a surprised but pleased smile Morag's way.

"Good job, Daria," Morag whispered, not wanting to startle them. "Now, tell them that Queen Cadha sent me. See if they know why. Or if they know any secret paths to town."

While Daria sang, Morag approached them cautiously. She knelt and extended a hand, whispering softly that she was sent from the queen.

The hares' ears twitched, their noses quivered, and something in their eyes seemed to acknowledge Daria's plea. One of the bolder hares hopped forward, its eyes fixed on Morag, and then turned, leading her toward a thicket.

With a swift glance behind, Morag quick-stepped after the hare. She hadn't intended to leave the castle grounds before consulting with the queen, but when else would Solly not be hanging around the garden?

"Shall I come, too?" Daria stood, the other hares still gathered inquisitively around her.

Morag raised a hand in farewell. "Nae, dear. You take the herbs back to the kitchen before anyone notices you're gone."

The hare led Morag to a concealed entrance hidden amongst the brambles and roots. The hare seemed to nod, as if encouraging her to proceed.

"Is the tunnel large enough for me to go in?" She asked indicating her height. While not as tall as the humans, she wasn't as small as a hare.

The hare hopped closer to the entrance, brushing aside some of the brambles to reveal the hole. It was just large enough for Morag to crawl through, as if made for her size. She should have known.

"I suspect you have many tunnels, and I don't want to get lost. I need to get across the river." She pointed toward the town. They waited, watching each other. "Do you understand me?" She pointed again. Hares and fairies did not share a language, but she hoped with Daria's introduction they would share an understanding.

The hare seemed to respond, its ears twitching once before it hopped into the tunnel, pausing inside the entrance to look back at her. Its dark eyes beckoned her onward.

With a deep breath, Morag got down on her hands and knees and followed. Her hands sank into the damp earth, the scent of moss and hidden life filling her nose. The passage was narrow, even for her small size to fit into, and she blocked most of the light coming from outside.

"Och, this is going to get dark, isn't it? Don't get too far ahead." The hare led the way, always just a leap in front, its soft tail visible in the dim light filtering from the tunnel entrance. Morag pulled her silver wand out of her pocket and, with a flick, caused all the surrounding roots to glow in a web of white veins. "That's better." She tucked up her kirtle to expose her knees for easier crawling.

Once underground, the tunnels were even larger than she expected, as if the animals had been preparing for a moment such as this. Still, if she were to take the babies out this way, she'd need a sled to pull them behind her. The way would be slow, but, as she examined the sturdy walls, safe.

The tunnel twisted and turned, a labyrinth beneath the earth, but Morag felt no fear. The hare's presence was comforting, its movements sure and purposeful.

Soon, the tunnel narrowed again and sloped sharply downward, the air growing cooler. The smells of damp earth gave way to something fresher. Morag's breaths came out in sharp puffs as she tried to keep up with the nimble hare. And even though her fingers brushed against the slick walls, feeling the occasional trickle of moisture, she trusted the hare, trusted the greater work around her.

The sound of the hare's feet on the packed earth changed, becoming softer. The ground beneath Morag's feet became wetter, and she realized they were approaching a part of the tunnel that must lie beneath the river itself.

She paused, the realization washing over her. The river that had seemed such an insurmountable barrier was now a mere ceiling of rock and water above her head. The hare stopped as well, turning to look at her, its ears erect.

"I hope you know what you're doing," she said.

In this deep place, the walls of the tunnel were smooth, glistening in the light of the tiny luminescent roots bound in these ancient peats. Through the ceiling came a distant, rhythmic sound, a muffled but powerful echo from the river's current above.

The hare inclined its head and, with a twitch of its ears, seemed to be encouraging her to continue.

She rubbed the sore area of her injured arm, working the stiff muscle. "Let's keep going." She focused on the hare's forward movement and ignored the disconcerting sounds. She was uncomfortable being so far underground—a fairy was meant to soar! But the wee bairns needed her, and the hare was willing to guide. The small were often overlooked, but together they were mighty when they each did their part.

After much crawling, they quickly began to ascend. Morag paused to flex her aching hands, but her knees bore the worst damage.

Finally, the light in the tunnel up ahead began to grow, and the hare stopped, turning to face her.

"Thank you, friend," Morag whispered, reaching out to touch its soft fur. The hare allowed the touch. "Wait for me? I willnae be long." *I hope.*

CHAPTER 10

ORPHANS

As Morag emerged through a thicket on the riverbank, the sun was already high in the sky. The passage had taken longer than she had estimated it would, and she still had to make the return journey.

"Och, my hands!" Pieces of peat clung to her palms, along with tiny pebbles and mud. She brushed them together before straightening her kirtle. The bottom half of her skirt looked like it had been dragged through the mud, which, of course, it had.

After tidying her appearance as much as she could, Morag set off for the narrow streets of the besieged town. While she wanted to take to the skies, she thought it best to not let word spread around town that a palace fairy had crossed the river. Osario would be on her in a minute.

It had been months since she'd last ventured beyond the castle grounds, and the grim reality of the standoff shocked her. The once-thriving market square was deserted, the stalls abandoned and covered in a fine layer of dust. She paused a moment to survey the scene. Her keen fairy senses picked up on the pervasive fear that had taken root in the hearts of the townspeople.

The top of the mercat cross in the center of the town square had been vandalized. The unicorn had been broken off and lay on its side at the base.

"Och, who would do such a thing?" Morag looked around as if expecting to find the culprit. "What is happening to this kingdom?"

She bent down to examine the statue and was relieved to find it was in one piece. Not undamaged, but mostly intact. Morag righted the unicorn figure and dusted it off. She heaved and lifted it, a shooting pain going down her weak arm. She fluttered up and down and up as she struggled to return the statue to the top of the mercat cross. Stone grated against stone as she set it in place. She dusted her hands. "There. As it should be."

She continued on, her worries escalating. As she made her way across the street and then into the alleys, she overheard snippets of troubling conversations behind closed doors.

"If we just surrender, they'll stop the attacks. Perhaps it's the best way."

"Brigid said her daughter is still missing. She was last seen near the river helping with the washing. We all know what that means."

Oh, aye, the kelpies have been up to no good. The townsfolk needed a palace fairy on this side of the Tarner, too. She'd have to let Mavis know how bad it was in town. As important as their presence was at the palace, so it was needed in town.

A thin man tipped his cap politely at her as he passed. He was completely unaware that a bogle with a large nose and pointed ears was walking right beside him, and the bogle grinned at her, pleased that it could exist in the same space as humans without them knowing. It was a good thing the humans didn't have eyes to see everything around them. This particular bogle was wiry and ugly and obviously looking to cause trouble.

In an alley behind a pub, a serious discussion caught her attention. She stopped to listen.

"They're not as monstrous as we've been led to believe. The king just wants us to think he is the only one who can save us. The big hero." The voice sounded familiar. Perhaps the official who talked to Lord Ewan at dinner was making good on his plans to stir things up.

"I agree. We need to think about the future, our children's future. We can't go on like this."

There was a loud thump, as if someone had slammed a full tankard onto a table.

"Enough of this!" a new voice said. "We won't bow down to them. Ever."

"We're just discussing—"

"Discussing? You're speaking of betrayal, of handing our kingdom over! Our ancestors built this land, were here before the kelpies invaded from their invisible realm, and I'd rather fight till my last breath than let those creatures claim it."

"It's not betrayal, Hagen. It's survival. What's the point of a kingdom if there's no one left to rule over?"

Ah, Hagen. He worked the town side of the bridge. A reasonable man, perhaps too proud of his thick mustache, and he was friendly with Osario.

"There'll be no kingdom if we give them what they claim to want. They want us gone, is what they want."

Morag shook her head as she moved on. *The fracturing has begun in earnest.* Once a faction had decided on the easy solution, it wouldn't take long for the shift to happen. Senna and the orphans needed to be away before any mobs had a chance to form.

"Morag! Thank heaven the king's let the palace fairies out." A jolly woman in a purple wool kirtle crossed the street with open arms, her face beaming.

"Hush." Morag waved her hands in front of herself trying to indicate discretion. "I've not been here. You don't see me," she said.

"Oh!" the woman's eyebrows rose, then she touched a finger to the side of her nose. "I'll not tell a soul." But she grinned and moved quickly down the street toward the bakery.

Either the woman would tell no one or tell everyone. Morag

couldn't sense which it was, only that the woman was all in on her decision. There was nothing Morag could do about it now, so she pressed on.

At the far edge of town, she found the mill Old Lennox had mentioned. It had become a sanctuary for the orphans. As one of the early mills, it used to have water flowing through its water wheel, but the tributary's path had changed and what was once riverbed was now a ravine and a future egress point for the children when it was time to go.

Morag peered into a dusty window. Inside, several children played games in an open space on the floor. Several others focused on quiet activities away from the action. Senna walked past and Morag quickly tapped on the glass.

Senna squinted through the panes. When she realized who it was, she opened the window and looked at Morag with a mixture of surprise and curiosity. "Morag! What brings ye here across the river?" Senna asked, her voice filled with concern. "Is it me da? Is he all right?"

"Your da is well, but I'm on Queen's business today." Morag waved her hands to stop Senna from jumping to any conclusions. "She is also fine, for now."

Senna's eyes took on a bit of mirth. "Did you see how blustery Osario got in the kitchen? I thought I'd see steam pouring out his ears if he'd continued any further."

Morag chuckled. "I'm pleased your plan to get yourself kicked out of the castle worked. You held steady and didnae wither under his gaze. You could have ended up in the dungeon the way you were pushing him in front of that junior guard."

Senna shook her head. "My father's position rescued me from that, I ken."

"You play your role too far, sometimes. It would be wise for you to learn discretion."

The lass's expression closed off, not expecting the rebuke. "What would the queen have with me, then?" she said.

"This is your warning. She wants you to take her bairns with you when you go."

At first Senna's eyes widened, then she smiled, jutting out a hip and setting her arms akimbo. "First, I'm kicked out of the castle for being a miscreant, and now the queen is going to trust me with her own wee'uns? Imagine that?" She laughed. "Does me da know?"

"If I know your da, he and the queen have been discussing options for quite some time now."

"Aye." Senna bit her lip as a flash of worry crossed her face. "What is it?"

"Approval from the queen doesnae change our situation with the kelpies. They're still blocking our way out, and ye ken we can't take the bairns up the mountain way. 'Tis not safe to travel right now, even if the queen wills it."

Morag nodded solemnly. "I ken, but your father and the queen believe it's the bairns' only chance. They have faith in your ability to guide the wee'uns to safety. And I will do everything I can to help you."

Senna took a deep breath, her resolve hardening. "As you say. I can be ready in a few weeks. Days? Och, Morag, ye don't mean today?" Senna's expression changed as Morag kept shaking her head.

"I don't think today, but the moment you hold those bairns, that is the time to set your feet to the path. You willnae get a warning."

A little boy with freckles and unruly brown hair broke away from the game he was playing with an older lad about Senna's age. He came running over, his face alight with curiosity. "Miss Senna, who you talking to?"

Senna smiled down at him, her countenance showing the boy there was nothing to worry about. "This is one of the palace fairies, a friend. Say hello."

The boy waved shyly at Morag, who returned the greeting.

"Now go back with the others," Senna said, spinning him

around. The boy reluctantly returned to the game. The older lad sitting at the table looked on with curiosity.

Curious, herself, Morag said, "I thought you were alone in your plans. I'm glad you have a laddie here to help. He must look older than he actually is, otherwise he would be training with the new recruits at the castle." She raised her eyebrows, hoping Senna would elaborate. Morag thought the older lad might be the blacksmith's missing apprentice.

Senna looked uncomfortable, revealing what Morag suspected. She let it go. "Be swift, lass. When it happens, the world is going to be a tumble."

Senna nodded, her eyes once again filled with determination. "Aye. We'll be ready." With a final nod, Senna closed the window and disappeared into the dimly lit room.

CHAPTER II

ULTIMATUM

When Morag crawled out of the tunnel back on the castle side of the river, she had expected the hare to return her to the Queen's Garden, but that's not where it took her. Instead, they ended up downstream at the very edge of the property.

"I'm too old for this," she muttered as she dusted off her hands again. The trip back had taken her longer to travel, and the stars were already out. Mavis and Solly would have questions she didn't want to answer. Especially Solly. After bringing flowers to the prince and princess, she'd know Morag hadn't returned to attend the queen.

Morag was about to mutter more to herself but realized she wasn't alone. The king and Osario stood with their backs to her, facing the river. She pressed into the thicket.

What are those two up to?

While she watched, a man emerged from the water. As he stepped onto the bank, moonlight glinted off his skin, illuminating him enough to reveal the tangled seaweed in his long, slick hair that fell like a mane; his body covered in algae. A shudder ran through Morag. A kelpie in its human form. They were loath to take the form, so whatever purpose it had here with the king was serious.

"You lied to me, mortal king," the kelpie said, his voice smooth but carrying a deadly undertone. "The prince of our blood is not here."

Morag gasped. She couldn't help herself. The king had told the kelpies that their prince was on the grounds! Och, why would he do that? No wonder they attacked the castle.

"I need more time." The king looked past the kelpie, as if expecting more of them to arrive. When no more came out of the river, he straightened his shoulders, appearing slightly larger, more commanding.

The kelpie, unnaturally stiff, said, "Relinquish our kin, lest your realm be washed away by our wrath." The kelpie's gaze darted between Osario and the king. "We demand his freedom, or ye shall pay dearly."

The king didn't flinch. "You can't kill me, because then you'd have to return to the invisible world. My protection allows you to live in our world in exchange for your strength to help us build and harvest. You cannae touch the authority of the land, and that authority is me."

"Long have we watched the likes of you rise and fall. The river remembers none of you. We could offer peace but would require royal blood in exchange."

"The bairns!" An excited cry came from the shadows near the river. Lord Ewan scrambled down the slope to the water's edge, seemingly oblivious to the shock registering on the king's face. "The royal bairns! They're only days old, barely alive, really. It's so simple. You'd be a fool not to agree."

Morag covered her mouth to keep from crying out. Would the king give up his children as the queen feared?

Seamus turned his back on Lord Ewan. "The best I can do is royal sheep. As many as you want from my own flocks."

So there was some humanity left in the king, after all. How

long could he hold up to the mounting pressure from advisers like Lord Ewan?

"You try my patience, mortal." The kelpie sneered, baring its teeth as a horse would. "But you won't live in this realm forever."

He stepped back toward the water, and that's when Morag noticed he had hooves like a horse instead of feet. She also noticed that the water from the river was receding ever so slowly. Slowly to a human's eyes, but at a faster rate than yesterday. The kelpie should be noticing, too, but the king and Osario had him distracted.

Osario stood silent, his hand resting on the hilt of his sword and his face menacing.

"The kingdom comes first," Seamus's voice was firm, resolute. "I have to do what is best."

"There is more than one way to get what we want."

A tense silence followed.

The kelpie's voice rumbled into the quiet. "Seamus, you are running out of time. Release our prince and return his magical bridle, or we shall bring ruin upon your kingdom. We no longer care about consequences."

Morag wondered. Did the kelpie speak the truth, or was it a bluff?

King Seamus remained quiet for an uncomfortably long time. Finally, he spoke. "You must know that my queen is ill. I cannae possibly do anything other than spend my time tending to her. You must be patient."

The kelpie laughed, and as if on cue, more kelpies in human form began to emerge from the flowing water, a small army standing waist deep at the river's edge. A low, collective growl sounded like the echo of distant thunder, their presence adding to the weight of the kelpie's threat. He took a step closer to the king. "We have been patient for generations of your kind. It ends with you."

King Seamus, instead of being cowed, seemed to take strength. He stood tall, his eyes hard as the granite of his castle walls, a flicker of defiance igniting within them as the kelpies left the water and surrounded him and Osario. "Do it now!" King Seamus commanded, his voice thundering across the landscape.

The words crackled in the air, and for a heartbeat, everything fell silent. Then a cascade of stock-and-horn blasts split the silence, a chain of them echoing up the river. Moments later, the churning waters came to an abrupt halt, the roar of the river replaced by an eerie silence. The once rushing waves slowly drained from the riverbed, leaving it bare and curiously exposed.

The king's risk paid off. The rivermen had been hard at work for weeks, but to see them actually stop the river was shocking. The exposed riverbed, rocky and coated with water weeds, revealed decades of discarded objects, broken tools, and even the decaying bones of a sunken boat.

A slow smile spread across the king's mouth as the kelpies' faces twisted in confusion. "How long is it that you can live out of water?" he asked. He signaled with an upheld hand as hidden guards descended onto the trapped kelpies. "Subdue them."

A mass of soldiers rushed past Morag, and she pressed farther into the shadows, holding her breath. Lord Ewan quickly retreated while Osario began to wrestle with the kelpie representative. The kelpie struggled violently against Osario. It pulled him into fighting in the middle of the riverbed, where the ground was alternately rocky, muddy, and slippery.

Because the kelpies needed the water to pull their strength in order to transform, they were fleeing to any remaining pools of water left behind.

You fools. Get out of there.

One kelpie found a pool large enough that it was able to transform into horse form. The soldier grappling with it immediately let go so as to not get attached to its sticky hide. Released, the kelpie galloped upstream while the rest continued to fight.

The guards, realizing they'd not been fast enough, pivoted back toward dry land. *Get out. Get out.* Morag willed them to move faster.

More of the king's guard descended, these carrying long poles with looped rope at the end, and others with claymores. The battle continued, as the guards with claymores cut away as many kelpie bridles as they could, while those with poles attempted to capture the stranded kelpies and prevent them from reaching water or running away.

A junior guard, looking somewhat confused and repulsed, collected and held the kelpie bridles away from his body. The magical bridles would later be stored in the deep archive in the castle.

In the distance rivulets trickled across the riverbed, growing louder and louder, joining together, flowing around rocks, then streaming over the rocks, building and racing toward the castle. Morag wondered if any of them apart from herself could hear the river breaking free. With a sudden ferocity, the dam upstream completely gave way, releasing a giant surge of water. The river roared back to life, a raging torrent unstoppable in its course.

The emptied riverbed flooded in mere moments, and the guards scrambled to get away from the water. But the waters continued to surge, chipping away at the banks, searching for equilibrium. There was a loud yell as one of the guards slipped, and the current tore him away. He was quickly lost downstream.

Morag took to the skies. No one noticed her, as they were all so focused on the chaos at the river. She flew as fast as she could downriver. She spotted the guard, fighting to keep his head above water. *Och, it would be you.* She recognized him as the blond-haired one who was with Osario the night he caught Senna stealing. The once confident, sneering young man was now desperately fighting for his life.

Up ahead, a tree leaned close to the bank, its roots recently exposed by the fast flow. Morag took out her wand and used her fairy magic to give it a little push. Instead, it broke off like she'd sheared it. The trunk went tumbling downstream, being no help to the struggling man, and she lost sight of him. She stared at her wand. *What is happening to me?*

Meanwhile, the kelpies' triumphant thunder echoed down the reclaimed river. In their horse form again, they ran wild and free away from the castle with the flow of the water. But then they turned and, in a demonstration of power, rode against the waves with a fierceness meant to intimidate the guards.

Osario directed every available guard to take their prisoners away. If the kelpies had won the recent battle at the bridge, the guards of Glenmoor won this river battle.

As the rushing water began to calm, the river returned to its regular banks. A group of guards made their way down the river-bank, trying to find the man lost to the river. They ran past Morag, not noticing her slumped against a tree stump. She listened as they sped away until she heard one of them shout, "I see him!"

Morag returned to the castle in time to watch the kelpie leader reemerge in human form. He remained in the river up to his waist, arms crossed. The king and his guard stood far back from the beach, up on the meadow.

"The kelpie prince is bound, but the river is free. If you think you can control the river in order to control us, you're mistaken. The river knows no mercy, and neither do we. Grant us what is ours in three days. That should be time enough to extract him from whence you've hidden him. Consider well, mortal king. Are thy children not sweet to thee? Think not that stone walls will protect thee, for the river flows through even the mightiest of castles. Our patience is not infinite. If you fail, we'll take one of your realm's younglings each day until you return our prince. Give them up willingly at the flat rock downstream, or we'll take all we will. Look to thy shores, king, and tell us—how many villages can you lose before your people despair?"

His haunting laughter chilled Morag's blood. The queen's instincts had been correct. Seamus was playing a dangerous game with the kelpies.

The kelpies disappeared as quickly as they had come. The king turned on his heel and strode back to the palace, Osario at his side, a fresh wound marring his face and a slight limp indicating he'd been hurt more than Morag had noticed. He'd be even more keen to rid the kingdom of the kelpies now.

Morag bit her lip, glancing back toward the river before daring to follow behind the men on foot with her wings tucked in tight. Still sore from her crawl underneath the river, she hobbled after them. *We must look a sight limping into the castle. All except the king. He looks none the worse for wear, standing back while his guard protected him.*

"I willnae give them the bridle," the king was saying. "I would sooner melt it down and wear it as a chain about me own neck than let that creature have it."

Osario stopped abruptly and Morag almost stepped into their view. She froze in place.

"You're not serious?" Osario questioned the king. "You don't know what that would do to you."

When the king didn't answer, Osario lunged to pull back the king's coat. The king dodged, shoving Osario, stumbling away. "You forget who I am. I am king and you obey me."

"Yes, sire." Osario took a demurred posture, his shoulders relaxed and his head lowered.

Seamus straightened his coat, then revealed his bare neck. "I havenae done so. It was simply one of the options I've considered. You don't know how many plans I've dreamed up and rejected." He resumed walking back to the castle, and Morag let them get far ahead of her before she followed. "Although that particular idea came from Lord Ewan. Clever fellow, but it's my neck to wear the bridle."

"You seem to be at an impasse. What are you going to do?"

"Wait and see how terrible their attack is while we stall for time. And if it's as bad as I suspect, in the end, I could release their prince." The king's tone was tinged with desperation as he weighed his options with Osario. "That beast is useless to me the way things are now. Do ye ken it would be enough to satisfy them?"

"Not likely. But it may be enough to give some relief to the people while we figure out what else to do."

"There is nothing else." The king pointed back at the river. "That was our best idea." He glanced around, then lowered his voice. "What of the orphans?"

"There are a large number of them." Osario spoke plainly, but he had to have known what the king was hinting at.

"Then we have time. One a day. It's better than the alternative."

"I'll go personally to choose…"

"No. I need you here. Send someone else."

"Aye."

As Morag watched Osario agree to the king's plan, she felt sick to her stomach. The king might believe he could outsmart the kelpies, but at what cost?

This should not be the price of peace.

CHAPTER 12

FAIRY CONFERENCE

Prior to the Kelpie Wars, there would have been music and dancing after dinner, but with the queen confined to her chambers and the constant strain of combat on the soldiers, night came early these days. Most of the castle's inhabitants, unaware of the king's attempted ambush and failure to stop the river, had already retired to their quarters. Only the fairies and a handful of maids were about, dousing the lights in the atrium.

"Where have you been all day?" Solly asked, the snuffer in her hand hovering above the candles on a wall sconce.

"Och, leave her be," interjected Mavis. "The way you two natter on sometimes. I'm not of a mind tonight." She doused the lights in front of her, further dimming the room.

But Solly would not be dissuaded. She followed after Mavis. "Morag's been avoiding me. She's up to something." She spun back around to Morag. Her eyes narrowed. "Her and Daria. You didn't think I would notice her waiting outside the garden, did you? You aren't trying to meddle in her life after accusing me of the verra same, are you?"

"The war is escalating—"

"Changing the subject again? Why don't you help us put out

the lights?" Solly moved on to another wall sconce. "Unless you've lost your snuffer."

Morag sighed. *Who needed a snuffer, anyway?* "The rivermen failed," Morag announced more forcefully. "They tried to hold back the waters and at first it worked. The king set his trap and lured them out. Dozens of kelpies in human form stepped out of the river and became stranded. The king's guard started to arrest them, when one escaped and managed to transform into a water horse. It must have made it up to the dam. Hardly a few minutes had passed when the river roared back to life."

Mavis stopped working. "I thought I heard a commotion," she said. "Not a surprise. I didn't figure the plan to begin with. Hold back the Tarner? They'd as soon move a mountain in Evermoor. I ken they tried moving a river once before, and it was moderately successful—"

In thought, she tapped her snuffer against her hand. "They must have him up there, near the headwaters at the bend for the dam. They'd need all the kelpie strength to cut off the flow of water that quickly. But I've looked, and there is no clear sign of exactly where the kelpie prince is being held. I've never been so frustrated."

As a demonstration of her frustration, Mavis stashed her snuffer in her pocket and began to pace three feet off the ground. She continued thinking out loud. "And probably also where they took the new captives. I'll have to slip away tomorrow and see what I can do about that prince."

"Och, but that's not the worst of it, Mavis." Morag held out her hand to stop the fairy's pacing. "The kelpies say they will take a bairn a day until the king releases their prince. And if the bairn isn't voluntarily surrendered, they will take what they will."

Solly balled her fists. "You mean they are forcing the king's hand to approve of the practice. Because there are children missing now. The kelpies are already taking them *now*." She turned to Mavis. "Shall I flee to the mountains for help?"

Mavis shook her head. "We need you here. The water pixies

will have to come." Mavis looked resolute. "We cannae save the kingdom without them."

Morag reached for the very important key around her neck, relieved that she still had it.

"Then who do we send?" With a glance at Morag, Solly tugged at the necklace around her own neck and pulled out her key, a compliment to the one Morag held tight.

"Daria." Morag whispered her name as she realized. Of course, it was Daria. *But then who will save the prince and princess?*

"Why do you say Daria?" asked Mavis. "The kitchen maid?"

"Aye," Morag answered with growing confidence. "She'll be able to speak to them, and they'll listen. She has the gift. None of us need go."

"But she's so young." Solly shook her head in disagreement. "Dare we send her out without our protection?"

"The closer she gets to the mountain, the safer she will be," Mavis said with conviction. "The pixies will know she's on her way, I'm sure of it."

"And how will she obtain permission to leave the castle?" Solly changed her voice to mimic the young maid. "Oh, king, I'm going to collect the pixies, yes the verra ones you hate and keep banished as your forefathers did." Solly returned to her normal voice. "Whereas I can simply fly away. The king only thinks he controls us, but we all know he doesn't."

"Hush, Solly. You're being indiscreet." Mavis held a finger to her lips.

"There is a way," Morag said quietly, glancing around, listening for anyone nearby. "Let's finish dousing the lights, and I'll tell you."

Mavis waved her bell-shaped snuffer and peered at Morag. "You look tired, dear. Best go straight up now."

"That's because she's been up to something—" started Solly, going back to the original topic.

"Grand idea, Mavis. I'm pure done in." Morag glared at Solly as she passed and even pinched her arm a tiny bit.

"Ouch!" Solly exaggerated the pain. "If you didn't want me to —OUCH!"

Morag pinched her again.

"Enough!" Mavis said. "I swear you two behave no better than the wee'uns around here. Solly, you take the lights in the eastern wing."

Solly leaned in so Mavis couldn't hear. "You're up to something, and I'm going to find out what it is. We're on the same side, ye ken."

"Stop." Mavis held up her hand, a concerned look on her face as she flew to Morag's side. "I know something has happened that worries you. Keep your part in it secret if you must, but tell us the rest tonight."

The palace fairies' room was at the top of the tallest tower, as far away from everyone as the king could get them. Their windows opened to allow them to fly in and out as needed. The top tower room contained Solly's collection of flame lilies (much to Mavis's chagrin) and Mavis's mirrors, including her time mirror, which revealed past or present depending on the phase of the moon. Morag's side of the room was stark in comparison. She liked to keep everything in her pockets, just in case.

While she waited, Morag stood in front of the time mirror wondering how it revealed information to Mavis. The mirror only worked for her, no matter how often Solly looked into it. Morag had long given up on seeing into the mirror, but thought she'd take a peek tonight just in case something was revealed to her. She saw nothing but her pensive reflection.

When finally, the other two slipped into the room and closed the door, the three fairies stood in a tight circle. Morag and Solly looked at Morag expectantly. She quickly filled them in on what happened at the river, then moved on to what they needed to do next.

"You know the holes that have been vexing you, Solly?" Morag said. "The hares have dug them, and their tunnels go right under the Tarner."

"I knew it." Solly pounded her fist. "Well, not the details, but I knew something important was underway. I tried to tell you, didn't I, Mavis? I tried to tell both of you, but neither of you stopped long enough for me to explain." Solly crossed her arms in an attempt to look irritated, but her smile gave her away. She was thrilled to be vindicated.

"Tunnels under the river...a hidden way out of the castle. You sought this path for the queen, didn't you? For the bairns?" Mavis was quick to see the plan. "So, Daria escapes that way and goes up to the mountain retreat for the water pixies. It's the closest one and the fastest for a human to get to through the portal. But will she do it? It will take courage to go through the forest."

"That, I don't know," Morag said.

"Could we get someone to go with her? Someone like that young guard?" Solly blinked innocently.

Mavis shook her head. "Osario would never allow it, not when every guard is so desperately needed here. Nor could the lad sneak off. We'd never get him alone long enough to explain why he should defy the king's orders." She shook her head again. "No, Daria must determine to go herself."

"And I must clear it with the queen," Morag said firmly, knowing the queen would not be pleased to have to change the plan. "Why don't you two prepare the supplies for Daria while I speak to Cadha?"

"Aye," said Mavis. "Then meet us in the archive room so we can pull a map for her. Surely Lennox will have a copy on hand."

CHAPTER 13

MIDNIGHT ACCUSATIONS

In the dark bedroom, Morag stared at the queen, willing her to wake up. She didn't feel right about sending Daria away without the queen's blessing, especially since doing so would interfere with the queen's more urgent task for Daria. Och, the poor lass had no idea how her future was being plotted around her. But that was the way of things, wasn't it?

The embers in the queen's fireplace glowed extra bright tonight. By their sparkle, Morag could tell the peats had come from the distant village of Brae. The diggings near the salt marsh were known for their special properties and were coveted throughout the kingdom.

Once Morag was done here, she'd meet up with Solly and Mavis in the archive room and wait for Lennox to produce a map for Daria. Solly could create the map herself, as she knew the way. Her key unlocked the particular hidden door that led to the fairy pools where the closest colony of water pixies lived, but Lennox was more detailed in his cartography. Solly went by feel and flowers and other changing landmarks such as the movements of honeybees, which were only helpful to herself.

The queen stirred and Morag leaned in, hopeful. "Majesty? Is that you awake?" When there was no answer, Morag shook the bed. A wiggle, really. But as the night nurse had her own sixth sense about her, time alone with the queen was short. The special nudges Morag had given to the night nurse and the nanny to leave the room would amount to nothing, and one or the other would be back in no time to check on the queen and the bairns. This conversation needed to be over by then.

"We must speak now. Sorry to disturb."

"Morag..." Cadha's response was barely a whisper. Her eyes remained closed. "What is it, Morag?" she mumbled, clearly not fully awake. Did Morag need her fully awake?

Morag leaned in close to the boy child. "Today he looks like an Eric. And she an Eileen."

The queen ignored their little game. "Did you find a way?"

"Aye. It's as the note suggested. The hares have dug tunnels under the river. I can get your bairns to Senna."

"Wonderful. But why...the sad...tone?"

"A new complication. We need Daria's assistance with gathering the water pixies. With your permission, we will send her out immediately."

The queen's eyes fluttered open. That got her attention.

"What's happened?"

"The attempt to divert the river failed." Morag left out the part about what the kelpies were threatening to do. No need to add to the queen's distress unless it became necessary.

"A diversion worked...in the past, other kingdoms. Fairloch. Have we lost...the knowledge? Lennox said..."

Cadha tried to push herself up, and Morag pressed her back down. "No need to get up and put a robe on. Just nod your approval, and I'll be off before your nurse returns and sees me here."

"But the bairns. Morag, what...will we...do with them?"

"I've not forgotten, and if need be, Mavis and Solly will fly them off at the last minute. I think that's the best course, anyway."

The queen frowned. Clearly, she disagreed.

Morag waited for the queen to wake up enough to think things through and come to the same reluctant conclusion she had.

"But...the lass...is so young. Lived her whole life...in the shelter of the palace, aye? Never in the...wilderness?" questioned the queen.

"Aye."

"And Solly...can't go because we need...her...here. For the...bairns. Same with Mavis. And I'm going...to send you...on your own...adventure." Working through the pain, Cadha sank farther into the pillow. "My thoughts are...so slow to...form, Morag. I'm...tired."

Indeed, Cadha's breathing was labored, with the faint trace of a disturbing rumble. Morag regretted disturbing her so late.

"I'm trusting you...to think through...the decisions for...me. Don't...steer me wrong, Morag."

"Nae, Queen. Ye ken I won't."

"Then do...what you think...is best. Report to me...as often as you...see fit." She reached out a hand and squeezed Morag's arm. "In no regard...spare me, Morag. I...want the...truth."

"Aye, Cadha. And ye shall have it." Disheartened, Morag stood to leave. The squeeze Cadha had given her was presumably to show Morag strength and determination, but the touch had been light, like the brush of a butterfly, so that it had the opposite effect. At the open doorway, Morag turned back, the light from the sitting room casting a beam across the bed. Cadha closed her eyes, her lashes glistening.

A lump formed in Morag's throat. A significant lump. She tried not to get too attached to the humans with their short lifespans, but Cadha had been different. Morag was attached, and her heart broke to see the queen suffer so.

Sure footsteps began to echo in the stone hallway, signaling that the overprotective nanny was returning. At a fast clip. Aye, an irate clip. Morag closed the door, flew up to the ceiling of the empty sitting room, and hovered in the darkest shadow she could find. She was in no mood to hear a lashing from the nanny, not when she agreed that the queen needed her sleep.

The nanny went straight to the queen's bedroom, pausing at the door. Without looking up, she said, "You best get yourself to the king's council chambers. They're gathering for an emergency meeting and they're about to hear from Lord Ewan. I know he's got it out for you." Then she entered the queen's room, closing the door silently behind her.

Morag sighed. If the nanny was warning her about a secret late-night meeting against her, the situation had to be serious.

IN THE KING'S council chamber, there was a hidden perch behind a grate atop a tapestry of the River Tarner. Back when the king welcomed the fairies, he liked for them to observe meetings and then later give him counsel. It had been years since Morag sat here, but there was no dust. Mavis was the one who kept up with the practice, whether or not the king still asked for the advice.

With a good view of the room below, Morag watched as Lord Ewan approached King Seamus. When she'd arrived, they had been discussing the failed attempt to stop the river, and Lord Ewan had been pacing the edges of the chamber waiting for his turn to speak.

The air was thick with tension, the usual chatter of the court silenced by the gravity of a midnight meeting. Candles flickered around the room, casting shadows and making even the friendliest face look rather ominous.

"My lord," began Lord Ewan, his voice oozing what Morag had come to recognize as feigned concern. "I stand before you with a matter most pressing regarding the safety of your kingdom and the loyalty of those within these walls."

King Seamus, his brow furrowed with the weight of an already trying day, leaned forward. "Get to the point, Ewan."

Morag tensed.

"It grieves me to say this," Ewan continued, his gaze flicking around the room as if to ensure confidentiality. "But I fear there may be traitors among us. More specifically, I speak of the palace fairies."

A murmur rippled through the chamber, and Morag felt a cold knot form in her stomach. The nursemaid had done her a good deed and the fairies would be in her debt.

"The fairies, you say?" King Seamus raised an eyebrow in skepticism. "They have been part of this castle for generations. A nuisance at times, but traitors? What evidence do you bring?"

Lord Ewan's lips curled into a sly smile. "Observations, my lord. But they are telling. The fairies seem to be everywhere, privy to all manner of conversations. One cannot help but wonder to whom they truly owe their allegiance. To you, my king, or to others with less noble intentions?"

Morag dug her fingernails into her arm to keep from crying out. The nerve of that man when he was the one sneaking behind the king's back, ready to strike.

"They are creatures of magic, unpredictable and not bound by our laws. In times such as these, can we truly afford to trust them?" Ewan pressed, his voice a blend of concern and insinuation. "In fact, the recent attacks should be concern enough. It's as if the kelpies know our every plan. How could they unless someone was passing on our secrets?"

He glanced up, and Morag froze, worried that the lighting might give her away. It may have done, as Ewan was now staring at the king, but with a smirk.

"One was even seen in town, even though you have forbidden them from leaving the grounds. You see how little they regard your commands."

Och, she had been noticed in town more than she realized. She doubted the woman outside the pub had given her up to Ewan, but maybe she had. She or someone else out on the street. Some things couldn't be helped and no use fretting over it now.

King Seamus pondered Ewan's words, his expression unreadable. Morag decided to act fast. She couldn't allow Ewan's poisonous words to take root. She extricated herself from the snug. Then, swooping down dramatically from the upper beams, Morag appeared before the king. The courtiers behind her gasped, as if she had confirmed Ewan's accusations of sneaking around. She cringed inwardly, chiding herself for taking Ewan's bait.

"Your Majesty," she began, her voice clear and unwavering. "I must speak. Lord Ewan's accusations are baseless and born of fear, not fact."

The king, taken aback by her sudden appearance, nodded for her to continue.

"We fairies serve this kingdom with loyalty and have done so for centuries. Our magic is used for protection and guidance, never for deceit or personal gain. To suggest otherwise is to misunderstand our very nature."

Lord Ewan interrupted. "The nature of the kelpies was to guard the waterways, until they turned on us. Who's to say the palace fairies haven't done the same? Already gone in league with the kelpies?"

Morag stared at Lord Ewan as murmurs spread through the crowd.

True, the kelpies' original purpose was to protect the waterways, the thin places between the seen and unseen, but they rebelled and entered the human world, seeking to control and cause havoc. They hated the high king and everything he loved. They were not content to live in their world, but wanted control in the human world, too.

King Seamus looked from Morag to Lord Ewan, the gears of thought turning behind his eyes. "I have always found the fairies to be loyal," he mused. "However, Ewan, if you have observations based on more than mere suspicion, you may bring your concerns to our regular council meeting. I think we all need rest before we reconvene."

As Lord Ewan bowed, he turned his head and cast a smug look in Morag's direction. He'd accomplished what he'd set out to do. Somehow, in the way Morag reacted, he was pleased. Again, Morag chided her carelessness. Just because her magic had gone wonky didn't mean her brain had to.

CHAPTER 14

OLD MAPS

The night was not yet done. Morag still needed to meet with the others. Daria needed that map before the sun rose and the castle came to life. She hoped the others hadn't been waiting long. With each passing moment, the tension rose, becoming a weight pressing down on her.

The archive room was located near the atrium beyond the great hall. Morag took the fastest way there, arriving at a closed door. When she tried the handle, the door swung open, already unlocked.

She did a quick sweep of the room. Scrolls and books filled the tall shelves and spilled out onto the floor. It was here that Lennox had spent his life, his mother before him, and his grandfather before her. Senna might have been the next archivist, except the girl was more suited to action than books and a pen.

Morag fluttered about the rows of shelves, looking for the others. Instead of the palace fairies, she found Old Lennox packing a satchel, hastily stuffing in parchment scrolls and a few old books. Good. He would know where the map was.

"Lennox, you've an early start to the day."

The old man startled, then relaxed when he realized who had

entered his domain. "Morag, I couldn't sleep once I determined what needed to be done. What brings you here?"

"I'm meeting Solly and Mavis. I'm surprised they're not here yet." What could be taking *them* so long? Daria could only bring a few items with her so she could move quickly and unhindered.

"You're the first, but I find this timing fortuitous. No need for me to go looking for the three of you, as I also need to speak with the collective." He pulled up a tall stool to sit at his drafting table. "Shall we wait for the others?"

"Aye, they'll be along shortly. But if you have a map of the foothills at hand, that would speed things along."

If Lennox was surprised at the request, he hid it well. A brief swallow and he was up and searching through a box of rolled maps. "I've only the one; may I make up a duplicate for you?"

"Whatever you think best."

"Not many request the foothills route, so I've no copies prepared." He pulled out a tightly rolled map, darkened with age, but still with clean edges, indicating a lack of use.

"How is the queen?" he asked as he spread the map on his drafting table. "I presume you checked in on her recently?"

"Her time is short, Lennox. Hours maybe."

Lennox nodded, a cloud passing over his face. He added smooth river-stone paperweights to the edges of the map to keep the sides from curling. "Even my human eyes can see that. We are her army that she is dispersing while she still can." He pawed through a tray of mapmaking tools and with the same exacting eye that Osario would choose a claymore, selected a writing implement. "She is a fine queen, and her passing will send the kingdom into terrible sorrow."

"We're already sorrowful, thems that know her."

He nodded curtly and tapped the table, refocusing. "Before Mavis gets here and declares everything a secret, will you tell me what this is all about?" He looked over the top of his reading glasses.

Morag laughed. Mavis did like to keep everything a secret. But this was Old Lennox. Of anyone in the kingdom, he'd figure it out on his own.

"We are invoking our treaty with the water pixies."

Lennox raised an eyebrow as he carefully drew the path Daria would take. "You fairies are leaving now? Is that wise?"

"Nae, we are sending a kitchen maid to unlock the door in the mountains."

He added markings to indicate a deep valley. "That's an unusual choice." Ever the diplomat, he waited for Morag to explain, not letting on that he was curious at all, though he had to be extremely curious at this point. As historian, he was curious about everything that happened in the kingdom. Especially when the event veered from the ordinary.

"It's not ideal, but we three are needed here, and yet we cannot defeat the kelpies without the water pixies."

"Speaking of releasing hidden objects..." His gaze darted to the window, then back to Morag. "There's something I've found in the oldest records of the kingdom." He leaned forward. "An artifact of great power, said to have the ability to restore our kingdom to what it once was. I assume you are aware of it?"

Morag studied his quizzical expression. Och, she wished Mavis were here to handle this question. She suspected Lennox was about to get very close to a hidden line and she didn't know how close she should let him get. She stared blankly at him. "What artifact is this?"

He reached for the satchel he'd been packing, his eyes intense. "The nature of the object is unclear. Some writers considered it nothing but a myth. But the more I read, the more I believe it to be real. I've been secretly researching its probable location for years now. With regard to our situation, I postulate that it is a deterrent that can be used in the river to make the water inhospitable to the kelpies."

"I know nothing of an artifact such as you describe," she said honestly.

"Or," Lennox held up a finger, "it has healing properties as yet undefined?"

Morag tried to keep her face expressionless but turned away as Lennox studied her reaction. Now, that kind of artifact she knew about. It was rare indeed. Lennox was getting closer to the truth. Events were moving rather quickly now, and nothing about the day was turning out as expected. *Och, where were the other fairies?*

"I don't hold much sway in supposed artifacts, Lennox. People will sell you anything if the price is right and the story halfway credible. Be careful."

"Aye, I've considered that," Lennox admitted, a desperate honesty in his voice. "But it's worth looking into."

"And you think you can find this artifact?" she asked, gripping the table. She didn't realize they were this far along in the timeline.

"I've found a hint to its location," he paused, drawing in a ragged breath. "I believe I know where it might be hidden, and that's where I plan to go next." He quirked a smile. "You wouldn't happen to know anything about that, would you?" He leaned forward, waiting for a response.

Morag flipped through a stack of parchments dating back to the first king, her thoughts focusing on the gaps in Lennox's knowledge and wondering how much she should fill in for him. Not that it would make much difference, but she didn't want the kelpies catching wind of any plans the high king might have. If Lennox were to get caught, with his deep knowledge of the kingdom, he'd be a fine prize for the kelpies.

Under his intense gaze, Morag relented a wee bit. "Aye, Lennox, and you are wise to pursue this path. That's all I'll say, so don't ask me more. Other than, be prepared for a great cost."

He offered a rueful smile, his eyes glinting with a mixture of fear and determination. "I've spent my life amongst dusty scrolls, watching everyone else go on adventures. I need to see if the myths I've been studying all these years could actually be true."

Morag nodded, already knowing they were true. "I understand, Old Lennox. Be careful."

"I will." He returned to his packing, a new vigor in his movements.

The faint rustle of wings heralded the arrival of the other fairies.

"Apologies for our tardiness," said Mavis. "Solly insisted we take care of something in our room first." Mavis gave Solly a side glance, but Solly grinned triumphantly.

Morag recognized that look. It meant one of Solly's harebrained ideas had turned out to be useful. Morag suppressed her own questions about what that idea might be. If Mavis wanted Lennox to know, she would have said so immediately.

"No matter. I'm almost done." Lennox slid the map so that the fairies could see his work.

Solly examined the map carefully. "Nicely drawn, Lennox." She pointed to a hill halfway to the mountain. "This is where the thistles grow thickest. You should mark that for Daria."

"Aye, good catch, Marisol." He leaned over and added a note.

Morag and Mavis exchanged a look over their bowed heads. Solly never minded when Lennox called her Marisol instead of Solly. And to be so polite in her feedback showed that the map was very good indeed.

"I'll let you add the exact location before you give Daria the map. And since I am also going to the mountains, I can go partway with her; see that the lass gets on the right holloway. That one, especially, may be too overgrown to see the path. I may even be able to provide her with a donkey to speed the journey."

"What?" Mavis and Solly said at the same time. "You're leaving?"

"Morag can fill you in after I'm gone." He marked the spot where he wanted to meet Daria. "I'll only wait until midmorning." He blew on the map and tested that the ink was dry with a press of his finger. With a glance at his dry fingertip, he rolled up the map and held it out to the three fairies.

Solly snatched it. "Thank you, Lennox."

"Now there is something I need you three to do." He gestured around the room, his hands sweeping over the endless piles of scrolls and ancient tomes. "This place... It contains our kingdom's past and present. Knowledge that is precious and dangerous. It must be protected. Can you lock the archives away while I'm gone?"

"You're asking us to protect the archives?" Morag tilted her head, eyes wide with realization. "You mean to seal them?"

"Yes," Lennox nodded, his gaze heavy. "I don't want anyone to tamper with these chronicles, and I've not had time to research everything." He pointed to his traveling bag. "I'm bringing several parchments that look to be copies, but the rest need protecting here."

Silence filled the room as the fairies considered his request. What Lennox was asking was no small task. The magic required to seal the room would be powerful, complex, and draining.

The old man sighed, leaning heavily on his desk. He peered at them one by one as the tension rose.

"Och, why not ask us for the moon?" Solly broke in. "That's a powerful magic, Lennox. The task will require all three of us to set it and later to break it, but Morag's abilities have been...in question lately." Solly's gaze flicked her way before going back to Lennox. "Are you certain of what you ask?"

"Aye. This room needs to be protected while I am away. Besides, you fairies live the longest. You can guard the knowledge in a way that I cannot."

Mavis joined in. "Lennox, the magic you're asking for... It's potent," she said, her voice filled with caution. "It's not something we fairies do lightly."

"I understand, all of you," Lennox's voice softened. "But I believe it's necessary." His words hung in the air between them, his face etched with determination.

"Very well," Mavis agreed. "We'll do it. But remember,

Lennox, once the seal is in place, it will only open for you or the combined presence of us three fairies. No one else can breach it."

Solly linked arms with Morag, as if eager to get started.

Lennox nodded, a mixture of relief and gratitude washing over his face. "Bless ye, fairies."

"What about the bairns?" Morag asked. "Can we allow them passage so long as their hearts are true?" She held Lennox's gaze. "In case we are not reunited as we are now."

Mavis agreed, as did Solly.

"You best leave us to it," Mavis said, handing Lennox his hat. "Morag, do you perchance have a hair clipping from the prince and princess?"

"Aye." From her pockets, she produced two tiny ribbon-tied bundles, pleased that she'd had the forethought, and that she hadn't lost them.

Lennox hoisted his satchel onto his shoulder. "Farewell, for now." He donned the hat and tipped it in their direction.

Morag hated to see him go. He was a vital part of the queen's secret society. The three waited for the door to close behind him before returning to their task.

"We ought to make a smaller room so no one asks questions," Mavis said, getting down to business. "We'll keep some of these basic texts out on display, and we'll start calling the room the library. Soon everyone will forget it was ever the archive room."

"Wait." Morag held up her hand. "What did Solly do that has her so triumphant?"

"I'll let Mavis answer." Solly grinned, blinking her eyes innocently.

Mavis stopped her fluttering and her expression grew serious, her brows furrowing. "She convinced me to look into the time mirror."

CHAPTER 15

SEAL THE ROOM

The time mirror. No wonder Solly was strutting. Mavis generally had a rule that if Solly asked her to use the mirror, that meant Mavis wasn't meant to look.

"What did you see?" Morag asked.

Mavis frowned. "The mirror's current phase is in the past. It showed me Lord Ewan, a man we've never trusted, and with good reason. Not only does his business rely on trade along the Tarner, but he is quite willing to make any deal the kelpies would give him. He held a meeting in the tavern just outside of town where he is amassing a large resistance to the king and in favor of the kelpies. I also saw a shadow hanging over the nursery, a sense of urgency we cannae ignore."

Solly's triumphal grin dimmed. "Ewan has the support of many. If they make a move on the castle, I don't know how Osario could hold them and the kelpies back."

"Then what do you suggest we do?" Morag asked.

"We do what is in front of us and then do the next thing. Ready?" She resumed her position in the middle of the room, her wand out.

"Wait," interrupted Morag, "Is there anything we ought to pull out of the archives and leave in a prominent spot?"

"You mean interfere?" said Solly in pretend shock.

"For the bairns. We don't know what the future holds, but Old Lennox, while strong of heart, is no longer strong of body. And Senna never took to the role, so she'll not replace him. I don't know who will. Lennox's replacement will need a nudge, don't you think?"

"Aye," agreed Mavis. "Let's each of us find a key document to leave on the bottom shelf over there. That shelf is unobtrusive, out of the way of a casual glance, but easily noticed by someone curious. It'll also be close enough to the barrier wall we'll create so that if we're not around, the prince and princess might touch the barrier and see that the room is bigger. Be quick about it. We need to send Daria on her way."

Mavis flew to the top of the highest bookshelf to begin her search. Solly went to the darkest, most mysterious-looking corner. And Morag started with the pile of parchments Old Lennox had left out, suspecting that these were the documents he thought important.

The documents on the table were old, fragile, and with curling edges. Documents that Morag had never seen. They spoke of the formation of the kingdom from a small settlement of sheepherders.

"These are from before we arrived," she said excitedly. "They're writings from Old Lennox's ancestors, from the kingdom's early interaction with the kelpies. But it's in the ancient text, which will make it hard for this generation to decipher."

"Let me see." Solly returned to the table and hovered over Morag's shoulder, and read aloud in short bursts:

"I saw the farmer Lachlan attend a kelpie in human form at water's edge. I was afar off and ran to rescue him, but before I got there, the two shook hands and the kelpie retreated into the river, transformed into horse form, and galloped away." She dropped the page and started with another. "This one is more interesting. It looks like a prophecy of the day the kelpies might rise against the kingdom."

"Och, we're already there, aren't we?" Mavis looked over Solly's shoulder. "Does it say anything else?"

Solly muttered aloud as she scanned the ancient text. "The blood of the throne will remain untouched." She looked up. "Is that good or bad?"

Morag pointed to the bottom, which looked like it had been torn off. "What is this part? Something about a bridle."

Solly squinted, trying to read the small script. "Aye. It's talking about something being bound. A protection, but the good part is missing. It doesn't make sense. We know how the kelpie bridles let them transform their shape, but this is a different use, something about looking through the rings. There aren't enough words here to know for sure what it's talking about. Maybe the rings reveal something like Mavis's mirrors do? I dinnae. Lennox might know more."

Morag left Solly and Mavis to scan through the documents while she stepped back and surveyed the room. She flew past the large family tree, noting that Lennox had sewn in lines for the names of the twin bairns underneath the union of Cadha and Seamus, but left them empty while awaiting the naming ceremony. Morag touched the empty spaces before she furtively used her wand to fill in the names. *Forgive me, Cadha, but I asked the wee bairns for the names you told them.* She wrote lightly, so that Mavis and Solly would have to look closely to notice. If everything went awry, at least there would be a record.

"Morag?" Solly called, making her jump. "Have we bored you? Let's get on with it."

"Just adding the hair clippings to the family tree." Morag slipped the tiny clippings into the tapestry.

Mavis made eye contact with each of them. "Ready?"

Taking a deep breath, Morag nodded and joined the other palace fairies. To her left, Solly practically glowed with excitement. It had been a while since they had joined forces to this extent. To Morag's right, Mavis hovered with her wings beating slowly and steadily, ready to make a section of the castle disappear.

They took out their silver wands. With a nod from Mavis, they circled the room, tracing a glittering cloud that spread out to the walls.

Morag, under pressure to perfect the sealing, wavered. Instead of strengthening the barrier, wild tendrils of magic darted out from her wand. The tendrils reached for one of the older books, pulling it off a shelf and causing it to burst open, its pages fluttering like in a strong wind. Another tendril danced erratically toward Lennox's table and one of the books he left out vanished.

"Morag, what's gone wrong with you now?" Solly's eyes opened wide, and she dropped her hands. "We'll have to start over."

Mavis put a hand on her shoulder. "I've noticed when your emotions get the best of you, your fairy magic...goes off a little."

"Kindly put, Mavis," Morag replied, her cheeks flushing with embarrassment. She had been emotional just then, thinking of the tragedy of the twins never knowing their mother.

Morag shot Solly a look. Solly shrugged, an amused twinkle in her eye.

"Shall we try again?" Mavis asked, her voice gentle.

They repeated the process, and this time, Morag took great pains to focus on the task at hand, visualizing the barrier's sealing and keeping her emotions in check.

The luminescent barrier seeped into the walls, floor, and ceiling of the room until it disappeared from sight. Despite being invisible, Morag felt its presence, a dormant power now part of the structure of the archive room.

"It's done," Mavis said, stopping to rest on the ground.

The archive room had shrunk to a small library, but there was a slight shimmer behind the walls, indicating there was more to the room.

"Remember not to stare," Mavis said as she led them out of the room. "We don't want to give any clues that this room is larger than it appears.

Meanwhile, Solly looked askance down the hall.

"What is it?" Morag said. She wasn't prepared to use any magic anytime soon.

"I think I saw a bogle."

"Here, in the castle?" Morag peered into the dim corners. "I saw one in town. I wonder if it's the same one."

"It's been a while since they've been active here," mused Mavis. "It portends a change, if nothing else."

"I hope it didn't notice what we were doing," Solly said as she looked back into the partially sealed room. "They like to cause trouble for trouble's sake."

"We won't know unless it acts," Mavis replied. "Be vigilant. And we should never go into this room together in case we accidentally cross the boundary, and someone notices we've disappeared into the larger archives." She closed the door tight. "Let's go wake Daria and send her on her way."

CHAPTER 16

THE KELPIE PRINCE

Four kitchen maids shared a dormitory, their sleeping forms mere lumps in the rustic beds. "Which one is her?" Solly whispered, a touch too loud.

Mavis flew around the room, eventually alighting on the small wardrobe cupboard beside Daria's sleeping form. She waved the others closer, and they gathered in tight.

"We're going to give her a fright, all of us staring down at her," Morag whispered. "Stand back and let me tell her. We have a rapport."

"Oh, do ye now," said Solly, not even trying to hide her irritation. "I thought *I* was the one who was *meddling* in the affairs of a kitchen maid and a guard."

"I never accused you, just asked about it. I knew you wanted to meddle, is all. You enjoy meddling when you can."

"Hush, you two. I don't know why you've been at odds lately."

Solly jutted out her chin. "Ever since Morag started keeping secrets from me."

"That's not fair, Solly. They're not my secrets to keep. They're the queen's."

"Even worse," said Solly. "Putting Cadha above me. A human."

"Only for a time. She'll not live much longer. She's *human*, after all. Today might be the day."

Solly dropped her jealousy. "I'm sorry, Morag. Truly, I am. Among humans, she is a gem."

One of the maids stopped her soft snoring and the three palace fairies froze. Mavis signaled to Solly to follow her, and the two flew up to the ceiling, leaving Morag alone with Daria.

Morag touched the lass's shoulder, giving her a shake. Daria rolled over and squinted in the dark. "What is it?" she said with a yawn.

"Get dressed quietly and meet me in the hallway. Take anything you deem precious as ye'll not be back for a time."

The lass nodded, though with a confused expression on her face. She swung her legs out of bed and startled when Mavis and Solly flew across the room to leave with Morag.

The fairies waited silently in the hall, exchanging all kinds of concerned looks. In moments, Daria joined them, dressed in her work clothes and with a small cloth bag slung over her shoulder. She closed the door gently and then looked at the fairies expectantly.

It was getting uncomfortably close to sunrise now, the glow beginning to warm the land, though human eyes would not register the change for another hour or so. There was a half-moon, so Daria would be able to see. With a grim face, Mavis led the way outside so they could talk freely. They stopped at the yew tree, away from the castle.

"We've a special mission for you, lass," said Morag.

"Do ye want me to speak to the hares again?"

"Nae, not that," Morag ignored the curious looks from the other fairies. "You are to go retrieve the water pixies and bring them back here. The archivist has drawn up a map for you, and Solly has a key that will unlock the door to their world. It's a portal, really. A shortcut that will make a week's journey in a blink of an eye."

Daria's eyes grew wide.

Solly took the key from around her neck and transferred it to Daria's. "The water pixies will welcome you, do not fear. And Old Lennox will meet you at the edge of town to walk with you part of the way and see you get on the right path. I've clearly marked the whortleberry patch, so look for it. It's a special one, providing berries in and out of season. Eat your fill because it's the last bit of food you'll get until you reach the pixies, and I fear their food portions are so small, even when they are being generous, you'll feel hungry."

Daria looked askance at Solly, so Morag jumped in. "We're sending you with provisions from the storehouse. You'll have plenty as long as you don't linger in pixie land."

"How far away are the water pixies? Does Cook know I'll be gone, or do I need to tell him?" Daria shook her head, as if trying to straighten out her thoughts.

Solly opened the map. "Don't fret. We've taken care of everything."

Daria's gaze wandered to the barracks. *Not everything,* Morag mused as she wondered, not for the first time, about Daria's young man.

Solly pointed the way. "Here is where you'll meet Old Lennox. He's in a hurry, so he'll only give you a few hours. If you miss him, just stick close to the map and you'll be fine."

Daria bit her lip. "I've never left Kingston before. Spent my whole life in the shadow of the castle until I moved here to work in the kitchens."

"Can't we send a guard with her?" Morag asked. She didn't like the hesitation she was sensing from the lass. Too much was riding on her swift travel. Osario would get over them requisitioning one of his men.

Daria brightened considerably at the thought, but Mavis shook her head. "Nae, you all know none can be spared. Not now.

Daria, lass, you will be fine. I've watched you. You're light on your feet. Efficient. And a quick thinker. You'll meet Lennox, and he'll get you halfway there. The other half, under Solly's directions, will be clear. Keep your wits about you, and you'll be back at the castle in no time."

Morag still sensed hesitation, even as the lass hiked up her bag and took the map from Solly. "Once you commit, Daria, you are a vital part of the plan, and we need you."

"You mean I can say nae?"

Mavis shot Morag a harsh look.

"Yes, lass, but we hope you don't."

The sound of an approaching barge came from the river, causing all three fairies to turn their attention to the landing. The sound was too quiet to garner human interest, but out-of-place enough to rouse a fairy's suspicions.

Daria didn't hear or notice the others on alert. "I'll do it," she said. "We all have to do our part."

"Hush, lass," Solly waved distractedly at her.

Mavis pushed Daria's head down. "Duck out of sight."

Goose bumps formed along Morag's arms, raising her alarms and sending her heart pounding. Something terrible was happening. She scanned the area until another faraway splash pinged her ears. As one, the fairies rose into the air and raced to the river.

They skimmed low over the castle grounds until Mavis pointed to another yew near the river's edge. All three crouched among the thick branches. From their vantage, they had a clear view of the riverbank below, where two figures stood in the pale light. Mavis and Solly kept still while Morag leaned forward slightly, squinting through the foliage. She recognized them immediately—King Seamus and Osario—their silhouettes tense as they faced each other.

Their conversation grew heated. Osario looked disturbed, his face a picture of grim resolve, while the king's face remained obscured in shadow. She edged forward, needing to hear clearly what they were whispering about.

However, their argument ended abruptly when a riverboat with tall sides arrived from downstream. By the clanging metallic sounds, she surmised the boat was coated with iron. She sucked in a breath. There was only one reason for such an action. They were bringing the kelpie prince back to the castle grounds.

"Nae," whispered Mavis. "I was so sure it were upstream! I've let us down. I wasnae able to get to the kelpie prince and now here it is afore us. I'll not be able to do anything helpful here. Not under the king's nose."

The large kelpie stood tall, unmoving. Its head rose above the unusually tall sides of the riverboat, making the guards nervous and twitchy. Its coat was so dark it nearly vanished into the night, save for a white star on its forehead that caught the moonlight.

Everyone on the river moved with great care, attempting to keep quiet. Thinking ahead, someone had spread straw about the deck to muffle steps, and there was no talking.

The first men off the boat bore stretchers. In all, six men being carted off were alive, though heavily bandaged. Three other stretchers indicated three deaths, their bodies fully covered with wool blankets.

Morag pressed closer into the tree, listening to the hushed whispers of the guards as the procession filed by.

"I'm glad I don't have to give a report to the king," one whispered. "There's ten more men we couldn't find. Pulled right down to the bottom of the river, I suspect. We'll be gathering up their entrails in the coming weeks."

When they passed her with one of the injured men on a stretcher, his hand fell out from under the blanket, and she recognized the braided leather bracelet he wore. *Daria's young guard! The one who bravely intervened for me. The girl will be crushed if she sees he's been hurt.*

Daria had remained where they'd left her, but she was peeking out from the bush Mavis had shoved her into. Hopefully, she was too far away to see that identifying bracelet. Or if she did, would be discreet in her reaction. There was no telling what Osario would do to the lass if he caught her watching this secret military maneuver.

Next came the guard leading the kelpie. Two handlers wore heavy leather gloves lined in the expensive kingdom silver. Still, they didn't touch the kelpie but led it with thick ropes. The others kept their distance, even though the kelpie wore the royal bridle and was therefore submissive to the king.

As Osario passed, his gaze ever watchful, he locked eyes on her. He gave her a disapproving look before continuing with his troops.

Och, that man.

The kingdom just got a whole lot more dangerous, and Osario knew it, too. Morag wanted to join the palace fairies and then go to the queen, but when she saw Osario's look, she knew she had to follow him instead.

"Morag," said Mavis, as she and Solly rose, "we must take to the skies and watch for a coming attack. Can you take care of Daria?"

"Nae," she said, her gaze following Osario. "I'm needed elsewhere as the queen's eyes and ears. Solly? Can you send the lass on her way?"

Morag would have liked to see her off as well, but Daria had all she needed. The hares would guide her safely under the river, and then Lennox would take her from there. Meanwhile, there were still things Morag had to do at the castle.

A faint sob came from Daria. *The lass did see. May she be more motivated to hurry to the water pixies.*

"I best go now," Solly said, looking hesitantly in the direction of the distraught kitchen maid.

"Aye. Help her best you can, and then send her on her way," Mavis instructed. With Solly gone, she turned to Morag. "We see the board being set, Morag. The prince returned, the king desperate...we know what must be protected. Tend to the queen's business. Solly and I will watch the river."

CHAPTER 17

OLD ENEMIES

Inside a large stable out of sight from the castle, the guards made quick work of securing the kelpie prince in a stall lined with iron. It was designed to conceal the location of a kelpie but with a cheaper material than kingdom silver. All the other stalls were empty. The horses had likely been moved out to the lower field, and the kelpies who had been captured when the river stopped could have already been loaded onto the barge to be taken upstream to work.

With the light from the sunrise beginning to shine through the open stable door, there was sufficient light to see well, especially for Morag. The windows had been shuttered, blocking the view of any curious passersby, but Morag knew how to get inside through a fairy door in the roof, fashioned back in the day when kings knew the fairies were helpers.

She sat high up on a corner rafter watching the entire proceeding. Most of the guards were visibly nervous and couldn't wait to get out of the building. When Osario alone remained, testing the chains one last time, Morag began to descend. But when the door opened, she quickly returned to her dark corner, tucking herself behind a beam.

It wasn't a returning guard, or a page looking for Osario. It was Lord Ewan, skulking inside, checking over his shoulder before sliding the stable door closed behind him. The room darkened.

If Osario was surprised to see him there, he didn't show it. "Lord Ewan," he said. He stepped away from the kelpie, not turning his back but taking several steps away.

"Osario." Lord Ewan stood close to the door, reluctant to get closer to the kelpie.

Good. From her vantage point, Morag could see the men as long as they didn't move closer to her hiding place.

The kelpie grunted, pawing at the ground. Lord Ewan would think it was irritated at being locked in the pen. Or, more pridefully, as being disturbed by his presence. But the kelpie prince was keeping its eyes on her, not the door and not Ewan.

She ignored the creature, though she was slightly pleased that she still had that effect on the kelpie prince even after all these years.

Lord Ewan whispered harshly, his words not hiding his irritation with the king. "I had heard the kelpie prince is back on castle grounds." He appraised the kelpie with an interested eye. "Wanted to see for myself."

Osario glanced around cautiously before speaking, his expression grim. "News travels fast."

"This is a dangerous game the king is playing," Lord Ewan said. "Holding the prince here will only incite the kelpies more. Or is this part of some greater plan to capture the rest of them and restore the entire herd to the kingdom?"

"The king believes he can use the prince as leverage, at the very least, to force the kelpies into submission." Osario's voice held a hint of disdain that Lord Ewan would surely pick up on. "He's underestimating their resolve."

"Then what is the king's plan?"

Morag clucked, loud enough to remind Osario that kelpies are not dumb beasts. One ought be circumspect around them.

"A demonstration." Osario's gaze flicked up and back to Lord

Ewan. He hesitated, as if gathering his thoughts before continuing. "On the one hand, he needs to show the kelpie prince has been treated well and on the other to show that their prince is domesticated."

Lord Ewan warily eyed the strength of the chains and the seeming disinterest of the kelpie. He turned, not quite putting his back to the beast, and pretended he was relaxed despite the sweat forming along his brow. "And what about the rest of the rumors? That the kelpies have been gathering in greater numbers? The kelpies know about moving the prince, don't they? Or they at least hoped their actions would press the king into taking this foolish action?"

"I suspect our riverboats are followed. We allow so few to travel the Tarner as it is, so when the king sent for the kelpie prince, there was a fight along the way. We won, barely."

At this, the kelpie snorted.

The stable door slid open just enough to admit the young guard who Osario had been keeping close at hand. His arm was in a sling after his tumble down the river, and he approached cautiously. But when he saw the kelpie well subdued, he gained the confidence of youth. His manner pinged all of Morag's senses and she rose, ready to intervene if needed.

"This is perfect," he said, his face a bit manic. "We can leave all the gates open. The kelpies escape and can leave our kingdom, and then the wars are over. Everyone wins." His hand shook as he reached for the latch.

Lord Ewan slapped his hand away. "Not so fast. Think about what we're giving up here. The kelpies, when domesticated, have helped us to build this great kingdom. We've grown faster and more prosperous than any surrounding nation. Besides, the king hasn't authorized you, has he?"

The young guard scowled. "If the king refuses to see reason, we must release *this* kelpie without his knowledge. Now might be our only chance to save ourselves. We can keep the others we've captured. It's the prince they want."

Osario's jaw tightened. "Hold steady. You're on the verge of being sent to the dungeon."

The young guard met his gaze squarely. "I'm aware of the risks. But you know the king doesn't have the will to let a single kelpie go. I say we free them all before our inaction leads to a disaster we cannot contain." He lifted his arm in the sling, wincing at the pain for effect.

If Lord Ewan had not been present, Osario may have treated the lad differently. But, like Senna, mistakes made in public had to be disciplined in public. In a kingdom on the brink of something no one was prepared for, everyone walked a narrow bridge.

"What are you here for, lad?" Osario said, throwing the boy a lifeline.

"You've been called to the council chamber. They're having a meeting."

"Aye, I'll be there shortly. Wait for me outside. You'll attend to me so you don't do something foolish."

Rebuked, the young guard nodded and left.

Lord Ewan had watched the exchange with interest. "You ken the kelpies are restless," he said. "Their attacks are more frequent, more...daring. I think we do need to take action before it's too late. I've tried talking with the king but to no avail."

Osario's response was tinged with frustration. "I've been managing the patrols, tightening security."

All true. Osario had been vigilant.

"And yet, your troops diminish with each attack." Lord Ewan pointed in the direction the wounded guard had gone.

"We're biding our time until the king has everything in place."

Lord Ewan snorted. "The king's plan—if you can call it that—is madness. Everything he does provokes them more." Lord Ewan's voice lowered further, forcing Morag to strain her ears. "The king has gone soft with the birth of those bairns. But I know him. He values his throne above all else. It shouldn't take much for us to sway him. You, his personal guard, and me, a most persuasive adviser."

"What do you suggest?"

"He's confused. Can't make a decision where those kelpies are concerned. He wants them stabled here, then he sends them away, then he brings back the one they want the most. He's going to destroy us all if we don't intervene. You know I'm right."

"If we can't sway him, we might need to consider alternative alliances. The kelpies are not mindless beasts. They want something. Perhaps a different negotiation is possible."

Negotiate with kelpies apart from the king? Morag couldn't believe what she was hearing. The idea was as dangerous as it was treasonous.

"A sacrifice should be sufficient to placate them. We can negotiate the frequency. They'll want one daily, I suppose, but that would decimate our population too quickly. Maybe one a month would be fine."

A vein pulsed in Osario's neck. "How many agree with you?"

"More than you'd guess. It's been the talk in town for weeks. Why don't I walk with you to the council meeting? I'll wait outside, but if you have an opportune moment, perhaps you can put in a word for me with Seamus?"

Osario was slow to answer. "Aye." With a slight pause and a nod. He opened the door. Lord Ewan scooted through first, eager to escape the presence of the kelpie. Osario followed, leaving Morag and the prince alone.

She flew down to the ground, gaze fixed on the kelpie prince. She stared at it for several heartbeats, trying to suss out its intentions, its demeanor.

"You willnae win," Morag whispered.

The kelpie barred its teeth at her.

"Grandstand all ye like. Ye know the truth. Ye are bound by the laws of the kingdom, as am I."

It swung its neck, catching the chain with a loud *clink*.

Satisfied, Morag left the stable. She needed to meet with the queen.

CHAPTER 18
THE QUEEN'S LAST REQUEST

A subdued sunrise shone through the queen's window, reflecting Morag's mood as she stood sentry in the queen's room. Outside, Mavis and Solly patrolled in the air above the castle with intensity. The sky was a swirl of gray clouds which cast an ominous pallor over the new day as if the heavens were preparing for the loss of the queen. Morag felt the weight of events with dread.

Far from the royal chambers, she'd heard quiet chatter that the rivermen were planning another way to divert the channel. But as she'd gotten closer to the queen's room, the tone had turned somber. The servants went about their duties as silent as walking trees. It was as if the entire castle held its breath in wait.

Morag hesitated to wake the queen again. She wanted a few more moments to set this peaceful view of the sleeping queen into her mind before upending their lives. These recent events had brought an urgency to them that left her no choice. Whatever the queen was planning, she needed to act now.

While she waited, Morag rubbed the sore spot on her arm, encouraging the blood flow and relaxing the muscles. If only she could fly like Mavis and Solly. She could be so much more help to the kingdom.

"Hello Morag," the queen said, her voice a vapor, an exhale. "Don't you...fairies ever...sleep?"

Morag stretched nonchalantly before moving closer to the queen's side. "Of course we sleep. Just not as much as humans."

Cadha let out a raspy breath as Morag sat in the chair near the bed. *How many more exhales did the queen have?*

"I see...another fairy, Morag. Did you...bring him?"

Morag glanced at the winged being who had been at the queen's bedside since Morag arrived. He was focused on the queen and the queen alone. Dressed in a white tunic, his arms rested at his side as if waiting, his wings at rest. "Nae, my queen. But do not fear the star. He is here to guide you home."

Cadha pushed herself up, fully alert now. There was desperation in her eyes, and she frantically patted around the bed, searching for her babies.

"They'll be here shortly," Morag said. "The nanny is changing them."

Cadha nodded slightly, such a sad look on her face that Morag wanted to cheer her up.

"The lad is looking like a James today, and the lass a Twila."

The queen settled back into her pillow. "I've already told them...their names, Morag, so you can...stop trying to sway me...to your choice for...their future."

"Tell us, then," Morag said, already knowing.

"Nae." She closed her eyes and smiled. "At the...naming...ceremony. It's...tradition."

"It's also tradition that the bairns hear their names for the first time at the ceremony."

Cadha's eyes opened...turned sad. "Aye. I started...a new...tradition."

"Then start another. A tell-the-palace-fairy-before-anyone-else tradition."

The queen burst out in a raspy laugh, going from sad to mirthful in a blink. So like her. Morag hesitantly grinned back, pleased to brighten the queen's countenance while she still could, but fearful of causing another debilitating cough. The figure hovering behind the queen also gave a slight smile.

"Nae, Morag. We both ken...how important...our traditions...are. They remind us...of who...we are."

"Och, so now you're a stickler for tradition? Even them that come from the mountain?"

The queen looked as if she were about to contradict Morag but stopped herself. "I believe, Morag. What you say...about the origins...of our kingdom. How the mountain kingdom of Evermoor..."

The door opened, and the nanny entered with the twins. She lit up when she saw Cadha awake, but her smile dimmed when she met Morag's eyes. She appeared not to see the third person in the room.

"Good morning," Morag said brightly. The jealousy between them over the children ought to stop. It was silly, and they needed to work together for everyone's sake. "Don't those wee'uns look well rested and content in your care?"

The nanny almost dropped the lass the final inches into Cadha's arms.

"Thank ye, Morag." Then, instead of stalling to stay in the room, she quickly excused herself and shut the door behind her.

"Well done," Cadha said with a raised eyebrow. "Mending fences...whilst you...can?"

"It's been a bit of a game with us, too, but I think we ought be serious for the time being."

Cadha bit her lip, reflecting. "Only we can...see...him?" She nodded toward the being at her bedside.

"Aye."

Nodding resolutely, Cadha continued, "So, tell me...why you are...here today."

"You already ken the plan to halt the river failed, but did ye know they've brought the kelpie prince back?"

Cadha breathed in deeply, as if to calm herself before speaking. "My husband...hated to move his most...precious belonging away. He thinks...he's controlling that kelpie, but I think we don't know...enough about them to be so...confident. What you've told me troubles me...greatly. I know I've not...long...to live, so now is my time...to act. To protect me bairns...and the kingdom, if I can. Ye ken the king is...too entwined with the kelpies. They've twisted...his mind and he cannae govern...wisely. It is time for your part...in my plan, Morag. It might be...the most dangerous...act of all. Are you...willing?"

Morag warily studied the queen, wondering what else Cadha had planned. "You want me to take the bairns, then? Now?" She hadn't secured a sled yet; so much had been going on since she returned. She'd need to gather nappies, food...food! She stared at Cadha. How were they going to feed the wee'uns without their mother's milk? Och, she didn't know half of what was needed. Maybe the nanny was better equipped for the task after all. Or perhaps a nanny and a palace fairy could care for the children together. Morag considered the prince and princess. They were so content, tucked close to their ailing mother. How could Morag even begin to care for them?

"Sorry Morag, I know you love them. But...now that you've...extended a hand of...friendship, it may not bother you so much...if our nanny is involved."

"Are you sure?" Morag tried not to scowl at the thought of the possessive nanny leaving the castle with an air of triumph. "She'll not be able to crawl through the tunnels, of that I can assure you."

"Nae, she couldn't make it...far on her knees, and not with...the bairns. I have an...idea that might work...to fool everyone, but the timing...must be...perfect. We have to let Osario take...the bairns to the...rock in the river...where the kelpies want..." She took a deep breath, unable to complete the sentence for the horror of it. "And at that...spot, with help from the...water pixies...they are coming, aren't they?"

"Daria should be on her way now."

"Good. Because...they will be able...to keep the kelpies at

bay...long enough for Senna...to rescue them." At this, she kissed each of their downy heads.

"Senna? But she's waiting for the bairns to come to her."

"Aye. In the chaos...that is about to happen, the bairns'...nanny can get her for me. I know she can. She has...a son in the guard...who won't stop her from...leaving the castle. And if the pixies don't arrive in time, Mavis and Solly can intervene. I know that I can trust my society of friends to protect...me bairns."

Morag noticed her name was missing from that list of protectors. What was it Cadha wanted her to do?

"Everyone must be...convinced that they each...got what they wanted...or someone else did...so no one goes looking for...me bairns. We can...spread conflicting rumors through...the town about what happened...to the prince and princess, and that will keep people...arguing amongst themselves and hinder...any rescue attempt they might...dream up. The king's advisers...will pick up on these...rumors and not be able to...discern the truth...either."

Morag examined the plan, thinking through the various possibilities. She could understand sowing confusion and spreading rumors. But tricking the kelpies was another problem. "I don't understand. How will the kelpies think they've won if they don't get the bairns? You aren't suggesting to use another woman's—"

"Nae, Morag! I could...never. They don't want...me bairns. Not really. There is something they want...more, and you'll be the one to give it...to them. Like the Pied Piper, you can use it to...lead them out...of the kingdom. Keep going...and never...come back."

"Their kelpie prince?" Morag shuddered inwardly. A big task, but if that was what the queen wanted, she would do it. She pictured the kelpies all thundering out of Glenmoor, but then the image turned to the kelpies with their prince turning around and decimating the land.

"Nae, we cannae...give them their prince," the queen said. "He is too well-guarded. Many people want...to set him free, so Osario...set up a round-the-clock guard...with instructions to cut off...the hand of anyone...who enters the perimeter in an attempt to...free it." She picked up her signet ring from her bedside table. She'd gotten so thin it would no longer stay on her finger. "My husband has...no idea of what a loyalist he has in...Osario."

"I'm of a double mind about releasing the beast myself. Once the kelpie prince is released, it would seek revenge."

"Aye. My thoughts, as well. Instead...you will lead...the rest of them out of...our kingdom, far enough...away that when...we cut off the water...again, they'll have to...switch to another source. We'll divide and...conquer."

"Of course. What would you have me do?" Morag dipped her head, wondering what kind of leverage the queen had over the kelpies.

Cadha took several moments to catch her breath and rally her strength. When she spoke, the words came without command, as if she had been wrestling with doubts. "Are you prepared...to leave...everything and everyone...behind?"

"My queen, I trust that you are not frivolous in your request. But I would rather stay with you until the end." A blue tinge to the queen's lips, seen by keen fairy eyes, told Morag all she needed to know. The humans would see the change in her soon, too. She was not long for this world.

"A few hours...or...days won't matter...for me, Morag. But you...must act...swiftly."

"Tell me what you'd have me do."

The queen then inclined her head toward the floor-to-ceiling unicorn tapestry beside the window. "Remove what's hidden...behind there...and take it...far, far away. I don't care...what you do with it, but...never let anyone...find it, ever again."

A thump sounded behind the door leading to the queen's sitting room. *So someone does listen closely, after all.*

Cadha startled, and she began a coughing fit, her eyes bulging and her face turning red. Instantly, the nanny came rushing in to help, bumping into Morag as they both reached for the water. *Where was the day nurse?*

Meanwhile, the princess stirred from her slumber beside the

queen and began crying. The nanny scooped her up and handed the lass to Morag. The lad remained asleep, and the nanny tucked a heavy feather pillow beside him to keep him from slipping off the bed while she focused on the queen.

Morag held the girl with her good arm. With the other, she reached into her pocket for something to entertain her with and found her candle snuffer. "There you are." She pulled it out, and the girl clumsily wrapped her thin fingers around it. "You already think everything is yours, do ye?" In response, the princess jerked her arm away and screeched all the more loudly. *Oh dear. The queen was right in not choosing me to sneak her bairns away.* Morag jiggled the child as she'd seen the nanny do many a time, to no avail. It looked so easy when someone else did it.

Meanwhile, the nanny administered a cup of water and rubbed the queen's back comfortingly until the fit had passed. "I have done as you asked, my queen," the nanny whispered, not realizing how keen Morag's ears were. "Me bags are packed, and I'm ready. So are the others. We'll be safe." The nanny glanced disapprovingly Morag's way as if to complain that Morag's lack of skill was disturbing the queen.

"The princess is settling nicely now," Morag said above the squalling. "Don't you worry about us."

In frustration, Morag took the lass to the window in the hope that Solly or Mavis would fly by and catch the princess's attention. "Hush now. You can't be causing a ruckus when your mam needs you to be silent. Oh, look, there goes Solly!" Morag did her best to distract the young princess, who blessedly stopped crying in an instant. "Hot and cold ye are," whispered Morag. But louder, she said, "There, now, that's better."

Morag grinned at the nanny. "Call me any time you need help settling the wee one. I seem to have the touch." The princess, while not looking contented, had at least stopped making any noise. Instead, her gaze was fixed on Morag, as if trying to make sense of her.

Morag gently bounced the lass near the window and the

princess closed her eyes against the bright light. Morag strained to listen for additional information, but the nanny said no more.

Everyone settled once again, the queen dismissed the nanny with a wave of her hand. With another annoyed look at Morag, the nanny left, closing the door quietly behind her.

"Well," Morag huffed. "I silenced the wee princess in the end. She ought be grateful."

The queen reached for her daughter, and Morag handed her over.

"You did a fine…job, Morag." When the princess was firmly back at her side, she said, "What of Osario?"

"Ah, a subject I am an expert on. He remains close to the king, and I sense nothing but loyalty from him."

Cadha pursed her lips. "What will the kingdom…look like when…all this is over, I…wonder?" She pointed at the tapestry. "Hurry now, and we'll say…our goodbyes."

"Och, what is it you have me do?" Morag flew to the tapestry, her gossamer wings barely stirring the air. She peered behind the woven fabric and discovered a small bundle wrapped in a faded cloth. Sensing what it was, the fairy's heart pounded in her chest.

"Nae, Queen."

"Are you…afeared? Now that the kelpie prince…is back…on the property…that cannae stay here. The two…cannae…come together. It's what my…husband and the kelpies are…fighting over. I wish that no one ever…lay eyes on it…again. And if it is not in…the kingdom, perhaps the kelpies will…follow you to…the ends of the earth. We need…to rid ourselves of them, and…I think we all know…that if we give them everything…they want, they'll…destroy us."

"I'm not afeared of the object." Morag twisted her fingers, thinking about all the objects she'd *misplaced* lately. "Wouldn't you rather set Mavis in charge of it?"

"Take no offense, Morag, but you…will be the least…suspected. Seamus will think…of a dozen others…before he thinks…of you."

And my presence least missed? Morag couldn't stop her downcast look.

"You are my...first choice, but if you...refuse, I will ask...another. Have faith, Morag. Isn't that...what you've always...taught me?"

"Aye. An ancient proverb. Faith is our hope, the evidence of what we cannae see."

Morag grasped the object in her good hand. With a grimace, she tucked it safely away in an inner pocket, loath to have it so close to her skin. "I have it now." She returned to the queen's bedside.

"Thank you, Morag. I trust...you."

"And the children?" Morag tweaked the lad's nose, and he sneezed.

"I know...that there are good...and true forces at work around us...and that they will...protect me bairns. I send you...away...with a plan. We mustnae...interfere until...my husband has made...his choice. Timing is...critical."

"As you say. I've enjoyed keeping time with you, my queen." Morag reached out and squeezed the queen's cool hand, wishing there was more she could do. Everything was going so terribly wrong.

Reluctantly, Morag backed away, solidifying the tableau of queen, prince, and princess all nestled together as it should be. On a whim, she selected a few silver objects from the queen's bureau: the silver hairbrush, a comb, and a handful of other trinkets. If she held more of the queen's objects that might disappear on her, perhaps she'd have a better chance of securing the one that mattered.

Morag looked to the queen for approval, but she'd already closed her eyes, her head tilted to snuggle against one of the bairns. The soft rattle in her breathing was alarming.

"Godspeed," Morag whispered to the queen, along with a glance at the being waiting nearby. And to the bairns, she said, "Until we meet again, prince and princess."

CHAPTER 19

THE BEGINNING OF THE END

Determined to live up to the queen's trust, Morag set to work. On her way through the queen's sitting room, she called out to the attendants with a little more bite in her tone than she intended. "Quit your lollygagging and do your duty. Attend your queen in her final moments."

They stared at her in shock and when the realization hit, burst into action. The eldest rushed to the queen's side. Another reached for smelling salts. Yet another for fresh cloths and a basin. Morag pointed to a vial of lavender water and the youngest attendant snatched it with a grateful nod to the palace fairy.

The attendants spent most of their days idle since the queen became bedridden. Their mouths busy with gossip and their eyes fixed on the handsome guards. They'd been waiting for this moment and would do honorably by the queen.

Using the utmost caution, Morag slipped through the shadows of the castle, avoiding the bustling corridors and the king's advisers who paced the halls, scheming their next move while the council met in chambers. Any misstep could lead to her capture and the exposure of the queen's plan.

She had almost reached the door to the outer courtyard when

she heard the echoing footsteps of the king approaching, along with someone else. *Och, the council meeting hadn't started yet.*

She tucked herself up into a darkened corner, hoping that the shadows would conceal her presence. The footsteps grew louder until the king appeared in the corridor with Osario.

The two parted ways, with the king coming toward her. His eyes scanned the area, and Morag's breath caught in her throat as his gaze locked onto her.

"You!" bellowed the king, his voice echoing through the hallway.

With a deep breath, she flew lower to face him.

"Why aren't you in chambers with the other fairies?" he demanded, his eyes narrowing in anger.

Morag hesitated for a moment, not wanting to point out that he never asked her to attend. As of late, he'd rarely even wanted Mavis there. "I'm running an errand for the queen, Your Majesty." She held up the objects she'd taken from the queen's vanity, thankful for that bit of foresight.

The king's gaze grew darker, and he took a step toward her. "Guilt clings to you like a shroud. What are you hiding?" he commanded, holding out his hand.

"The queen's silver needs polishing," she said, handing over an intricate comb to the king and ignoring the other object shoved into her inside pocket. "She's..." Morag debated what to tell the king. He knew that she was ill; aye, his use of the word shroud revealed where his mind was, but did he know that today might be the day? He ought to visit the queen to discuss the bairns' future and say any other words that needed to be said between husband and wife.

"She's what?" he bellowed.

Morag jumped. "She's sleeping peacefully."

The king examined the object, his eyes scrutinizing every detail. Morag held still, biting the inside of her lip while she waited. Apparently satisfied, the king grunted and tossed the comb back to her.

"Very well," he said dismissively. "And remember I want you lot to stay out of everyone's way. I don't want you fairies going around being a distraction. Lord Ewan has it out for you, and I'm not so sure he's wrong. If you don't at least pretend to obey my orders, I'll eject you all from my kingdom. Now join me in the council chambers."

MORAG PERCHED DISCREETLY beside Mavis in the shadowy upper reaches of the room. She watched with growing unease as the weary guards stood before the king, still in their armor, as if expecting another attack at any moment. Their armor was dented and stained with the evidence of a brutal encounter.

"Solly will join us shortly," Mavis said.

"What of Daria?" Morag whispered, leaning in conspiratorially even though no one could hear a fairy whisper.

"The lass is understandably upset," Mavis answered. "She saw her guard being taken away on that stretcher, poor thing. It's a lot for her to process."

"But is she off?" Morag pressed, no time for sentimentality. Her heart beat against the hidden object she had tucked into the inside pocket of her kirtle. She needed to be off herself. Once the king was distracted, perhaps she could slip away.

"Aye, the clever lass called to the hares, and they led her underground."

After the door closed behind the last council member, King Seamus, his face a mask of fury, rose to confront the guards.

"What happened out there? Explain how the kelpies could have known what we were doing," the king demanded, his voice echoing through the hall.

One guard, struggling to stand upright, answered through gritted teeth, "Your Majesty, it was as if the kelpies knew our every move. They were waiting for us."

The room fell into a tense silence. King Seamus's gaze swept across the faces of his courtiers, searching, suspecting. His eyes stopped on Solly, who had just entered the hall, her hands still dirty from tending to the garden.

Lord Ewan stepped forward, his voice smooth but laced with malice. "Might I suggest, again, Your Majesty, that the fairies are the problem? That one," he jerked his head in Solly's direction, "spends much time alone in the garden which is nearest the Tarner. Who knows what she might overhear while in the castle, and then relay when she is supposedly tending the garden?"

A murmur rippled through the assembly. Morag felt a surge of protectiveness for her fellow fairy. Solly's dedication to the garden was well known, but to twist it into something nefarious was outrageous. And where was Osario? He could be a balance to Lord Ewan. *Och, how fast a tide can turn.* She reached for Mavis's hand.

King Seamus's eyes narrowed. "Marisol, is it possible that you inadvertently gave away sensitive information?" He'd always had a softer spot for Solly, since he, too, enjoyed a bit of gardening now and then.

Solly, taken aback, stammered her response. "Your Majesty, I promise, I have done nothing but care for the gardens...both the queen's and yours," she said with a curious emphasis. "I've had no contact with the kelpies."

Lord Ewan's voice dripped with feigned concern. "But Your Majesty, we cannot ignore the possibility. The fairies' abilities are beyond our understanding. It's prudent to consider every angle."

"You'll never know what the palace fairies have done for you," Mavis said in their defense.

Morag's heart raced. She knew Solly was innocent, yet Lord Ewan's words carried a dangerous weight. The king appeared troubled, his thoughts weighing heavily on him.

"Until we have more clarity, the palace fairies ought be detained and questioned," King Seamus finally declared. "We cannot take any chances. Guards? Apprehend them."

The room erupted in more murmurs, and heads swiveled to watch the spectacle.

But before any of the guards could move, one of the queen's young attendants burst into the room, breathing heavy. "Come quick! It's the queen."

The king pointed his guards to the fairies as he strode out of the room, a determined look on his face.

Mavis tossed a pinch of sparkling dust from her pocket, causing the guards to shield their eyes and the room to darken. Then she flew away, snuffing out the candles as she went, adding to the confusion.

"You best get to the queen while you can." Solly gave Morag a little push. "I'll cover for you if anyone comes around to check on us."

Morag hesitated. Solly didn't know Morag was going to leave the kingdom. She reached out and hugged her friend tight. "You've always been so good to me."

Solly flustered. "Of course. Now off you go. It's going to be a long day."

"Solly, listen carefully," Morag whispered. "The queen wants you and Mavis to be ready to fly her bairns to safety if her plan fails."

"Morag, what plan? Tell us what you can. We won't let Cadha down."

"I only know my part, Solly, just trust me. I have to leave. Work with the water pixies to save her bairns but let no one know what you are doing. Let the drama play out as long as ye can stand it! You'll know if you have to intervene."

"What about you?" Solly called as Morag shot out the door.

Och, she hoped Solly and Mavis could put the remaining pieces together as they saw events unfold. Morag dared not say anything else with so many people around, even in a fairy whisper. But Mavis had picked up on so much of it already, she was likely already forming her own backup plans.

Morag raced outside and took to the skies, her wings beating furiously as she flew toward the queen's tower. After dismissing Daria's sentimentality, she had to indulge her own. Just one more look to confirm the queen was gone.

Fortunately, the curtains, though drawn, were cracked apart just enough for her to peer inside. Candles had been lit around the room, their tiny flames flickering like jewels atop the silver candlesticks and casting a warm glow. The strong scent of beeswax wafted outside, and Morag hoped no one would notice the open window.

As she approached the scene, she could see the lifeless form of the queen lying on her bed, her attendants silently mourning their lost monarch. Her heart lurched. The queen she loved so dearly was indeed gone.

King Seamus stood at the foot of the queen's bed, his face ashen. The room was filled with a deep emptiness left behind by the queen's passing and the bairns' removal. He gripped the edge of the bedpost, knuckles white, as if trying to ground himself in this new reality. Morag was surprised at his show of emotion.

Beside the queen's bed, one of the young attendants, washed over by grief, held the edge of the queen's gown, sobbing silently. Curiously, there was no sign of the senior attendants, the day or night nurse, nor the nanny.

King Seamus looked up, noticing the displays of emotion from the attendants, and straightened his shoulders. "Out!" He dismissed the mourners, claiming he needed a final moment alone with his wife.

The room fell silent as the door closed, leaving the king alone with the lifeless form of the queen. Morag's heart ached for him, and for a moment, she forgot their differences and simply grieved with him.

However, instead of paying his final respects, King Seamus released his grip from the bedpost and strode straight to the tapestry that adorned the wall of the chamber. He pulled it back, revealing the hidden alcove.

Morag held her breath as the king's expression shifted from confusion to disbelief to fear.

He reached in as if touching the empty space would make the bridle reappear. He flung the tapestry back over the hiding place. "Where is the bridle? Who has taken it?" he roared. The castle's stone walls seemed to reflect his anger, echoing back the urgency in his questions.

Morag hovered in place outside the window, a mix of fear and curiosity urging her to stay and watch. The king continued his tirade.

"That Lennox!" he snarled, pacing the room.

Och, Lennox had been notably absent at the council meeting. He usually sat near the front, recording the proceedings.

Morag looked toward the mountain road, wondering if Lennox and Daria had connected. He had been wise in reading Seamus's movements. Hopefully, he didn't plan to stop to say goodbye to Senna.

As the archivist, people gave him a certain amount of leeway, lest he write badly about them. He would use that to wend his way out of the kingdom, but once the king issued his decree, Lennox would be hunted.

While the king was pacing, a wind gust slipped through the open window and blew out the nearby candles. He jerked his head up in suspicion.

Morag immediately dropped below his view, hoping he didn't see her. Steady footsteps sounded closer, followed by a swish of the curtain. Morag could sense him fuming as he stared out over his kingdom. While she struggled to keep her movements as still as possible, a plaintive cry came from inside the room. Morag recognized the prince at once. One of the attendants must have brought in the bairns. *Och, a mistake.*

The king moved away from the window. "Get them out of here! I can't think when they're making that noise."

Concerned, Morag returned to the window, ready to intervene. The king had widened the gap in the curtain, and she could easily see into the room now.

The young attendant pursed her lips. "Yir their faither. They be needin' you the day. The princess is normally the squally one when she's upset, but verra sweet the rest of the time, like she is now. The lad is as even-keeled as I've ever seen, 'ceptin right now as he's missing his mam already."

Morag flinched. The attendant thought she was helping but overstepped her bounds. Where was the nanny?

"The bairns are my weakness, don't you understand?" The king turned his back and Morag was too slow. He saw her. And someone to vent his anger on.

He charged at the window. "I've had it with you meddling fairies. Secretly plotting with my wife. Telling her lies. Well, no more. I want you out of here. All of you. I don't care if it's tradition or if you offer us some kind of protection. I don't need you. I don't want you."

He threw open the window and threw a vase at Morag. "You're helping Lennox, aren't you?"

Morag, used to the king's outbursts, was quicker on her flight than she had been the last time the king threw something at her, and she dodged the vessel, hearing it shatter on the cobblestone walkway below.

When he reached for more projectiles, she darted upward.

"Guards!" Seamus yelled as she flew away. "Search the castle. Find me Lennox and that bridle. And bring me those fairies!"

CHAPTER 20

MORAG'S ESCAPE

It felt like every eye was on her as Morag made her way through the castle. Some of the servants who hadn't heard the king's edict yet stopped and bowed respectfully as she flew by. The laundress she'd spoken to earlier, one of the marshal's clerks, and even the steward. *Of all the days, why are they noticing me now?*

Flying through the atrium, she found Mavis consoling a group of weeping palace maids. Word about the queen was spreading fast. The edict from the king would be swift to follow.

"Mavis!" Morag flew to her.

"Excuse me lasses," Mavis said as Morag pulled her up high into the darkest part of the rafters.

"The king has discovered the bridle is missing, and he's called for Lennox and us to be brought to him. Find Solly and stay out of sight." She patted her pocket. "The queen has asked me to lead the kelpies away."

Mavis's eyes opened wide, and then her gaze fell to Morag's injured side. She set her lips, as if thinking for a moment. "Go. Trust that the queen knew what she was doing. Solly and I will make sure the bairns are safe and no one knows what happened to you."

"Thank ye, Mavis. It's a complicated ruse. They'll never stop looking for the bairns if you just take them away. The prince with his birthmark will be difficult to hide."

"Aye. We'll be ready for our part in it. Our timing will be perfect. Together, our little society will sow as much confusion as possible and take the focus away from the bairns." She grinned slyly, which was unusual for Mavis. "We can spread some shiny distractions and conflicting tales about a certain valuable object. Those who seek to harm won't know what happened. And if we are especially clever, even the kelpies won't know the truth."

Morag nodded her agreement. "Thank you. Tell Solly I said goodbye. I don't know when we'll meet again."

"But we will meet again." Mavis squeezed Morag's hands, and then they went their separate ways.

Morag left the castle at the first door she came across, leading out of the royal quarters. Out onto a group of guards spreading out protectively around the grounds.

Morag fumbled over whether she should make eye contact or ignore them completely. Which would seem more natural and not hint that she was hiding the most sought-after object in the kingdom? She did both. A quick glance that felt like she'd revealed everything, and then she scurried off like a guilty child. *Och, I'm not cut out for secrets.* She was sure Osario, supervising the lot, looked at her suspiciously. At least he might have. Would he have guessed that she'd come from the queen's room and was now trying to escape the castle grounds without anyone knowing?

Morag continued, head down, to the Queen's Garden, having sneaked past any who would stop her for conversation. Though, outside of Solly and Mavis, it seemed there weren't many. Since the queen had taken ill, she'd spent so much time with her that other relationships had fallen away. She moved freely past servants who didn't even look at her, perhaps assuming she would brush them off, anyway.

As far as she could plan, she thought it best to get to the other side of the river. She could go down to where the washerwomen worked at the river and then attract the kelpies' attention by showing them that she had the bridle they wanted. That way, she'd avoid letting the king know that she was the one with the bridle. She didn't want two enemies tracking her down.

The garden was empty, with most of the servants cleaning up after breakfast or off on other duties. Morag immediately went to the hidden tunnel entrance to make her escape. She'd think about where she was going during the long crawl to the other side of the river. Her movements were soft, barely a whisper against the damp earth. So several minutes in, when she heard a distant rumbling, it struck her as odd. The noise grew louder, morphing into an ominous groan that filled the tunnel, and then a small clump of dirt struck her on the head. She paused to reassess. Maybe she should have waited for a hare escort. When nothing else happened, she tentatively continued on.

More dirt and small rocks began to rain down from the tunnel ceiling. The walls shuddered, and for a second, Morag froze, eyes widened. Then her instinct for survival kicked in, and she turned back the way she came, her small form darting through the convoluted maze as the world around her disintegrated.

Dirt pelted her on all sides. Debris landed on her head, her arms, covered her legs. But she didn't panic until she tasted dirt in her mouth. She scrambled back into the garden just as the tunnel collapsed, the earth swallowing itself in a slow, winding path coming toward her, revealing where the tunnels were.

It could have been no coincidence that as she was trying to leave with the kelpie bridle her way of escape was blocked. As she stood, she dusted herself off, then with the first *clink* of chain mail sounding behind her, she dove for cover behind a large sweetbriar bush.

Peering cautiously from her hiding spot, her eyes narrowed at the sight that met her. Osario and his guardsmen were inside the Queen's Garden. Their weapons pounded into the ground above the tunnels. They had caused the collapse, a chain reaction.

While to Morag's distant left, the river raged, its waters

churning and frothing, indicating the kelpies were also causing a disturbance aimed at striking terror into the citizenry. This would only add more pressure on the king to act.

With the queen no longer able to protect her children, how long would it take for the king to come to the conclusion his heirs were expendable? Would Lord Ewan get in his ear, or would desperation be the driving force? How could she leave the wee things now?

Osario's eyes met hers for a brief second, and in that moment, Morag felt an inexplicable chill. His face showed no emotion, no sign of recognition, as he ordered his men to continue spearing the ground.

Scooting farther back into her hiding spot, Morag touched the bridle to assure herself she still had it, her mind racing for a new plan. The tunnels were no longer accessible, and time was running out. She had to act while Osario kept the guards busy destroying her escape route.

Morag slowly turned around and pushed deeper into the hedge, hoping to sneak through the King's Garden. But as she emerged, she found herself in a secluded plot that seemed wholly alien to the peaceful space of the Queen's Garden. The air here was dense with humidity, the plants crowding one another and fighting for survival. Vines of deep purple and maroon snaked across the ground, growing large thorns and strange bulbous fruits.

This was no ordinary garden; this was the king's poison garden.

Och, what Solly had to put up with.

Refocusing, Morag quickly ran through her options to lead the kelpies away. Since the kelpies seemed poised to strike now while the kingdom entered mourning for the queen, and if the king was despondent enough to make a rash decision, the children were in immediate danger. But to save them, she had to get rid of the threat.

Leaving those babies exposed was going to be the hardest

thing that Morag had ever done. To trust that the queen prepared her plan well. That Morag's task was the correct one. To trust others to do their parts. And for them to trust her, despite her lack as of late.

Morag realized she needed to draw as many kelpies as she could and lead them as far away as the ocean, if she could make it. But just yesterday, she could barely get across the river.

A rustle in the bushes startled her as a bird emerged, one wing bent and flopping on the ground. Such a sad sight. "You and me both, mother bird." When one of the castle cats also emerged from the bushes, the answer suddenly dawned on Morag. She shot into the air. "You blessed thing! Thank ye."

Morag's damaged wing was just the trap to spring on the kelpies. She could flutter from tree to tree, resting as needed, keeping out of their reach but also making them think they could get her if they were patient enough. It was the only way to give everyone the time they needed to rescue the babies and attempt to close off the river again.

For this to work, she'd have to wait until the twins were brought out to the flat rock in the river. There would be witnesses to spark the rumor that the kelpies took them. If anyone saw Daria's escape carrying her bundles, that would spark another rumor of the babies going off toward the mountains. And then, when the moment was right, she'd wave the bridle at the kelpies and lead them away, toward the ocean.

Since the queen had set her plan in motion, a palace fairy wasn't the only thing that was about to go missing. If rumors circulated that it was Morag who fled the castle, attention would be drawn her way. If she did this right, the others could complete their tasks with less scrutiny. Morag clutched the hidden object tighter, a surge of determination flooding through her as she slipped back into the Queen's Garden. Osario had departed with his guardsmen, leaving the Queen's Garden in shambles. Morag settled up into the tallest tree to watch and wait.

CHAPTER 21

THE CHASE IS ON

Midmorning, Osario held the prince and princess in his arms as he left the castle by the front door, not a secretive side door as Morag had been expecting. Och, the honor he gave the prince and princess to go out the front door as royalty with no shame or cowardice. No one was around to witness the event but Morag. Cadha would be pleased, at least for this moment in her children's lives.

And where were Solly and Mavis? They ought to be near. Ready to intervene. The flutter of a wing high up on the roof drew her attention. *Mavis.* Morag breathed a sigh of relief. Ever-dependable Mavis. *Never fear, Cadha. We'll protect your bairns.*

Now it was her turn to create confusion.

First, she flew low toward a line of laundry set out to dry. She picked off two undertunics with a silent request for forgiveness and formed the shapes of two bundles about the size of the wee bairns.

The laundress came out the door and caught her leaving. "Oi, instead of stealing my laundry, why aren't you getting rid of these kelpies?" She waved her fist at Morag. "What good is your magic if you don't use it? The king ought to send the lot of you back to Evermoor."

How quickly loyalties waned. Morag sighed. With no time to explain, she'd have to let the laundress work it out on her own.

Morag circled back and found a group of guards standing around as if waiting for orders. When they spotted her, she feigned surprise and darted off in another direction. They gave chase, but she quickly lost them. She had to make as many people as possible see her going in a variety of directions. If folks argued over which direction she was going, she could mask her true destination.

If only she could find Lord Ewan and make him think she was in the process of thwarting him, she could divert the attention of his resistance group at the same time. *Och, where is that sneaky man?*

Her intuition told her he'd be near the king, the last place she wanted to go. But, if so, then Ewan would already know that Osario took the children. Morag's thoughts swirled as she put herself in Ewan's mindset. He would want to witness the twins being sacrificed to the kelpies. He'd be following Osario.

Morag shot down to the river, looking for a man skulking in the bushes. There. Predictable as the freshets in spring. Ewan was staying far enough away that Osario wouldn't know he was being followed. Which meant Morag had a chance. She furtively got between him and Osario and then doubled back, flying upriver like she'd just rescued the bairns.

She flew low toward the bushes, looking backward like she was being chased. In her peripheral vision, she watched shock register on Lord Ewan's face, and she kept going like she hadn't seen him. Then she turned around and angled toward the bridge to town, making him think she was going that way.

Once she was out of his sight, she flew straight to the stables, stuffing the undertunics into her pocket.

To her relief, there were only two guards on duty at the stables. More importantly, one of them was the one she was hoping for. To the other, she said, "Osario wants you on the main door to the castle. They're expecting a breach and he wants the queen's body well guarded."

The dutiful guard nodded and immediately left for his new post.

As soon as he was out of sight, she turned to the other guard. "If you're going to release the kelpie prince, now is your chance. I'll turn my back for but a moment and deny any knowledge. Just be careful how you take off the royal bridle. Do so from above so it can't reach you."

The lad's expression registered shock. He began to speak, "I never..." Her message dawning on the lad, he immediately fumbled with the latch on the door and then slipped inside.

Morag planned her escape as best she could. She was already tired and would need to rest sooner than she wanted to. She had a few fairy tricks in her pocket that would help shield her if the kelpies got too close.

It wasn't long before she heard the last latch unbolt inside and, moments later, the impetuous guard screamed in pain.

Och, lad. Ye didnae heed my warning.

The kelpie prince burst out of the stable, barely stopping to take in its surroundings. For a moment, Morag thought she'd have to wave the cursed bridle at it to make it notice her. But then it stopped short. Surveying the land, its menacing gaze locked on Morag. Blood dripped from its mouth as the kelpie prince bared its teeth.

Morag put her hands on her hips. "Yes, I have your bridle. It's time you leave this kingdom and bring all of your followers with you."

The kelpie prince threw back its head and let out a shriek. Then it lunged after her.

She flew to the nearest tree, taking a brief respite on a solid branch. The kelpie prince ran directly for the trunk. *Thunk.* The whole tree shook, nearly unseating her. She fluttered off, trying to find other kelpies along the way.

Meanwhile, the kelpie prince dove for the water, reveling in its freedom.

Adrenaline surging, Morag flew along the riverbank before stopping to rest in a large beech. She needed to pace herself.

In the river, the kelpie prince ran with the water, trumpeting its release and gathering the kelpies for her. Six, seven, a dozen and more. Excellent. The kelpies kept emerging from the water until there were more bodies than water.

Morag set off again, staying just in front of the kelpies, but out of their immediate reach. The iron grates the rivermen had added to the river slowed the kelpies down as they had to either change form to slip through (those who had their bridles) or leave the river to go around.

The kelpies would be loathe to leave Glenmoor of their own volition, but Morag suspected she could at least lead them away from the capital and keep them busy for years. The queen had asked too much of her, not realizing Morag's limitations nor the kelpies full intent. How many of them would continue to track her, and how many could she entice into fairy pools where she could trap them? Teasing them with the bridle was the best she could do. And do her best, she would.

She flew past the flat rock where Osario was to leave the children. He hadn't arrived yet, and if she wasn't mistaken, she'd glimpsed Solly's round eyes keeping watch. Morag faltered in the air, dipping dangerously close to the river, and hopefully drawing the kelpies' attention away from Solly's hidden position. Water splashed up against her legs and the hot breath of a kelpie dried it on the spot. She shot up again, out of the kelpies' reach.

One tried to speak, its words garbled. It was probably best Morag didn't know what it said. In horse form, the kelpies spoke only reluctantly, for it was difficult for them to form the words.

As the rock left her view, Osario descended the bank. He'd had to cross the bridge to get to the rock, and that had taken him some time.

Morag glanced back again. *That's it. Follow me, kelpies. I have what you really want.*

They continued like this for miles, Morag dipping near the water when they seemed to be losing interest, then bursting ahead so she could rest in a tree. With a long way yet to go, she gave herself a few extra minutes of rest time, letting the kelpies circle below while she dangled her legs on a branch and rested her wings.

The kelpies circled and circled, and too late, she realized they were forming a rising whirlpool. The water propelled them higher and higher.

As she took off again, the kelpies rose to her height. The kelpie prince, leading the herd, snapped at her good wing. She winced in pain as teeth scraped along her side but got away from its reach.

The incident was a painful reminder that she couldn't let her guard down, not for a second. She'd almost forgotten that the kelpies could manipulate the river that way.

Several days after leaving the castle, Morag could barely keep her eyes open, let alone fly high enough above the trees. She was truly like an injured bird flapping from one tree branch to another.

She began to move in unpredictable paths, following the smaller burns, even those that were a trickle, far up into the hills and forests, looking for a place to stash the bridle in case her energy failed and they managed to pull her into the water.

The path she took was laborious, but necessary for her plan. As she went, she tore off bits of the cloth which bound the bridle and wrapped them around the pieces of kingdom silver she'd taken from the queen's room before tucking them into places high enough that the kelpies would struggle to try to get to them. She hoped that whatever magic was in the bridle left a residual scent or pull that attracted the kelpies. That way, if they got her in the end, they'd have to revisit all the potential nooks and crannies in which she may have stashed the bridle and waste a lot of time trying to find it.

Were they *all* following her? It was hard to tell, but it seemed so, as there were so many they jostled against one another in the narrow burn she'd gone up, away from the Tarner. They could sense her weakness, and all wanted to be there for the demise of one of the palace fairies.

She rested her head against the rough bark of a pine tree and weighed her options. If she continued like this, the kelpies would win. She hated to do it, but maybe the rings in the bridle could reveal something to her, as Solly supposed from the text in the archive room.

Morag took out the bridle, and the kelpie below her suddenly perked its ears. "I'm not tossing it down to ye, if that's what you think," she said.

Now she'd have to start all over with her hiding-place deception. She'd have to go back toward Kingston and revisit the trail of silver she'd left behind so they wouldn't know her final choice.

To the casual observer, the bridle was a simple construction of leather straps and silver rings. There were some etchings in the leather, kelpie markings. But the power was in the silver rings. At first glance, they looked the same as kingdom silver, but upon closer inspection, Morag recognized the other-worldliness of it. They were slightly darker, the inside of the rings especially, and warm with a subtle energy.

She lifted one up to her eye and peered through it to see what it would reveal. She drew in a sharp breath. Bogles all around, in the trees and on the ground, staying hidden from her natural view. And in the distance, past the trees that blocked her regular vision, she could clearly see more kelpies upriver, waiting for her return to the Tarner.

Och, but there was more to behold through the ring. Deep underground, bright white veins of kingdom silver snaked across the land. She could use that to her advantage. The kingdom's silver would slow the kelpies, draining them of their strength. All she had to do was lead them over the thickest veins and have her rests there. While her strength returned, theirs would be weakened. Pleased with her new plan, Morag returned the bridle to her pocket.

If only Solly were here. She would enjoy gaining the upper hand over the kelpies.

Morag set off again, deliberately leading the kelpies to a valley awash with underground silver. She nestled into a pine tree, leaned against the trunk, and immediately fell asleep. When she woke, she took the time to enjoy the thick pine scent and feel the sun warming her face before looking down at the kelpies. There were fewer there than she'd led to the spot, some of them wise to her ways. But the ones who stayed were laying sluggishly on the banks of the burn, their legs in contact with the water, but their bodies heavy and weighed down, bellies in the mud.

Och, better than I expected. With renewed strength, Morag continued on, leading the kelpies out of the kingdom.

At midday, she spied a hollow tree that was close enough to the river that the kelpies could be triggered by the location, but would not easily find it, given their limitations. Her plan involved a balance of keeping them interested, but not successful. She didn't want them to give up and go back to Kingston. If she timed everything right, she could keep moving the location and keep them occupied for decades.

After making several deposits of silver pieces into other nooks in the area, she circled back, paying careful attention to the foliage near the hollow tree, especially the clusters of snow drops whose blossoms would shine bright under the moon. She'd come back to this location under cover of darkness one night to leave the bridle behind. Until then, Morag returned to the river to taunt the kelpies and keep them engaged.

THEY'D BEEN FOLLOWING her for seven weeks now. Where the wee prince and princess were, she could only guess. But Mavis and Solly would need more time. So would the rivermen trying to cut off the kelpies' ability to return up the Tarner.

There had not been any veins of kingdom silver for two days now and she was near exhaustion again. She needed to sleep before she got too clumsy. The water was over her head before she realized how low she'd flown. The kelpies had stirred up the water again to reach her. The closest one snapped at her kirtle to bring her down but clamped too hard and bit off the wool. She shot up, dazed, into the air and safety.

It was time for her to hide the bridle for real.

"You'll not get me that easily," she shouted over the roar of the water. Her voice came out stronger and more confident than she felt.

Soon they came to a section of rapids followed by a waterfall and a pooling of the river with multiple burns feeding into it. The majority of kelpies waited in the pooled water while only one followed her down each burn. She'd set her pattern enough that they were getting lazy. That night, she left this kelpie far behind and circled back to the hollowed-out trunk she'd scouted earlier. The hiding place was easy to get to by flying straight across the land instead of following the path of the river.

She took out the bundle and nestled it deep into the trunk, covering it with several layers of moss and mildewy leaves. Then she was back to the Tarner in no time, making sure the kelpie prince saw her before setting out again.

She grinned when she heard it follow behind her. A part of her had worried that they would realize what she was doing. But even if they did, she'd left them so many places to look, they'd be busy for a long time. She'd be able to slip back and retrieve the bridle for a better storage place long before they found it.

CHAPTER 22
NEW BEGINNINGS

The village was smaller than most.

Crannogs, round thatched dwellings on stilts, dotted the landscape so that it was difficult to tell how many there were at the edge of this salt marsh. Morag had already visited three such places in as many weeks and hoped that this was the one. She was tired and really ought to slip away to the hollow tree, retrieve the bridle, and disappear into the wild.

She'd left most of the kelpies scattered, many isolated in fairy pools or lakes that wouldn't have egress until the spring freshets began to flow. The few kelpies who still followed her would be occupied for years, given the false clues Morag and Solly were leaving around the kingdom.

According to information Morag gleaned from a village closer to the capital, Mavis and Solly (Solly in particular) had taken great delight in handing out pieces of silver, including large rings resembling those used in bridles. The palace fairies had gifted the silver items to families in need and spread a rumor that the Kelpie bridle had been melted down and repurposed. The kelpies wouldn't know what type of silver an object was—kingdom silver or their own—until they touched it.

And as for what happened to the royal heirs, the tales were

many. No one had a definitive explanation about what happened after the queen died. The tales agreed only that the prince and princess were no longer at the castle.

Morag felt she owed it to Cadha to see for herself that the children were properly cared for. The princess had been placed with a woman in the village Morag had visited yesterday. The woman was older than Morag would have liked for the princess, but doted on her, nevertheless.

The prince was likely to be here, in this nearby village. Senna would want the twins close to each other in case of an emergency. Morag had to know for sure, so she hid herself behind a roof and focused on the town's square.

Several women met at the well to fill their jars and pass the news of the day near the mercat cross.

"The Kingston children are fitting in quite well, aren't they?"

"Aye. And now we've enough to start a proper school."

Small children from Kingston played around the square with the local children while adoptive parents looked on.

Morag waited, hoping for more folk to gather, but when none did, she secretly made her way around the village. She eventually found Senna organizing builders as they worked on new crannogs, swatting at the midges when the swarms were too thick. This land would not be an easy one to live in.

Now, where was the prince? Morag flew along the outskirts of the village, from rooftop to bush to the odd tree that managed to grow in this boggy land, trying to remain hidden.

"He's on the island," came a deep voice, causing Morag to jump.

She turned to see a grinning Osario leaning against a wooden skiff at the edge of the water. She barely recognized him out of his guard's uniform and wearing a riverman's tunic, let alone the smile.

"Is that safe?" she asked, squinting out across the marsh spreading out behind him. The water was heavily seeded with bog myrtle and glasswort.

"It's salt water and home to a new colony of water pixies, much to the delight of the village children."

"Aye, good. The kelpies' hides can't tolerate the salt." Morag nodded. "I don't see any pixies. Where are they all?" She continued squinting, looking for the tiny creatures.

"They didnae arrive in full force. Seems they only sent a contingent to balance out the kelpies. However, there are more of them here than you realize. You can see them better at night."

"Och, there goes one." A pixie zipped low across the water and disappeared in an instant behind a patch of bog myrtle. Seeing the pixies out in the open confirmed that Daria had been successful. "I still think there should be more."

"That's all they sent us."

"I'm grateful for these, at least." The prince and princess were safe, for now. "Cadha would be pleased. Did your part go well?"

Osario sighed. "In the end." He shook his head sadly and plucked a tall piece of grass. "Cadha didn't give me an easy part to play. My friend Seamus is not the man he used to be. I doubt he will ever forgive me for betraying him." Osario tore the grass into bits as he talked. "I brought the bairns to the river like he asked me to. A kelpie was already there, watching. Once I'd made eye contact with Solly, I gently placed the bairns on the rock. Said to the kelpie, 'There. The king has fulfilled your request. Now leave our kingdom.' Then I walked away, my heart pounding so hard I thought it would betray my true intentions."

Morag nodded. "I know what you mean. We all had to trust one another to not fail."

"Aye. And for the rest, you'll have to ask Solly. I don't know how she did what she did, but she met Senna at some point, and as you can see, we all made it here. We did not lose any of the children we brought with us. And they all have hope for their future."

"Should the bairns be kept apart like this? Who is watching over the princess if both you and Senna are here?"

"There are many things we haven't decided yet. Do we keep them on the move or let them settle in? Do we tell them who they are, or let them grow up not knowing? Do we keep them apart or together? Do Senna or I even stay once they are settled? At the moment, they are safe. We will adjust as need be."

For the first time since Morag had left Kingston, she felt a burden lift. The activities of the others had been as shadowy as a moonless night to her. She should have known that they were being just as thoughtful as she was trying to be. Which reminded her of the day of her departure from the castle.

"Osario, of all things, why did you try to collapse the tunnels with me in them?"

"Sorry if I gave you a fright, Morag, but the kelpies were patrolling the other side of the river, as if they were expecting you. They would have got you the moment you emerged unawares on the other side."

Morag remembered the dirt falling on her head. "Maybe a verbal warning the next time?"

"Oh, you plan on going underground again?" He said it with a relaxed smile, and Morag realized that, for him, too, the immediate danger was over.

"And how are things in Kingston?" she asked.

"When I left, the kelpies were all gone. The rivermen are continuing to muck up the river to dissuade them from coming back, erecting barriers downstream now that the water level is so low. They are committed to being better prepared for the next time."

"And the king?"

"I dared not return to find out. Ye ken I'm not his favorite person. I obeyed him to the letter, but by spirit to the queen. This allowed me to act according to conscience and the way the ancients wrote for us. Act justly. Love mercy. Walk humbly. I could not allow innocent life to be sacrificed."

"Aye. Words to live by." Morag waited for Osario to continue. She could tell by his face there was something on his mind. When he didn't, she prompted him. "What else, Osario? My time here is short."

"I'm not holding anything back. It's just suspicion, is all. I don't have your intuition, but I feel like the king has been hiding something from me. It's a mystery I'm trying to work through about the kelpies. While we've learned more about them, they've learned more about us. I fear something has changed and the king knows about it."

Morag nodded. "Makes sense. Mavis would know more than me. She can get closer to the king than I." She shrugged her right shoulder as proof and prepared her wings to fly.

Osario held up a hand. "Morag, do you think the kelpies will leave us alone out here?"

"I cannae say for sure, but you have all the protections we could come up with. I'll keep them chasing me for as long as I can. I promised their mother."

"Aye. Those bairns are the queen's hidden legacy. We will protect them with our lives."

Morag heard a noise and angled her head. "There's a wagon coming this way." She flew up for a better view. "It's a vardo, and from the sounds of it, filled with wee'uns."

"Aye, more orphans gathered from around the kingdom. As much as we tried to keep things quiet, word got out that a group was taking orphans out to the marshes. The folks here have been welcoming, and none of them know who we've mixed in amongst them. The woman who has taken in the lass is well pleased with her contented nature. The lad, on the other hand, seems more discontent. Sickly even. Did ye see the birthmark? Och, I wish that wasn't there."

"May I see him before I go?"

"If you've the time." Osario stared in the direction of the Tarner as if expecting trouble. The river was considerably lower than it used to be, making it much more difficult for the kelpies to travel and terrorize the way they used to. But the kelpie prince was out there, beyond the marsh and the tree line, waiting for her. She'd kept it angry and focused on chasing her instead of terrorizing the people.

"Aye, you're right. I've overstayed my welcome as it is." Morag pumped her shoulders, warming up for another long flight. "Thank ye, Osario. Don't tell Senna I stopped in. She likes to be independent, and I wouldn't want her thinking I don't trust her."

At that, Osario laughed. A good-hearted chuckle. "That lass has some fire in her bones, don't she?"

"Aye. Goodbye, Osario."

Pleased that everyone was accounted for, Morag continued on her way. Her role in keeping the kingdom wasn't over. Senna and Osario had the heirs secured, but she needed a more permanent solution for the Kelpie bridle. It was safe where it was for now, but she could take it inland, away from any rivers.

In her nonchalant, meandering way, she returned to the Tarner. She fluttered from one side of the stream to the other, randomly gathering herbs. The kelpie prince was hard to find, waiting just below the surface. *Och, there ye are. Dug yourself into the deepest pool you could.*

Once she'd spotted it, she kept her distance and fluttered awkwardly upriver to find a burn she'd not yet traveled along. By the time she'd found one, she'd attracted a significant group of kelpies who appeared rested and ready to track her afresh. Her heart sank. This was going to take longer and be more involved than she thought.

"I'll never tire," she called out to them with as much enthusiasm as she could muster. The thundering response below her rumbled deep into her chest and spurred her on. She'd bring them on a grand adventure, all right. See if she couldn't get them into one of the new tributaries that led away from civilization.

THE WEATHER HAD TURNED DREADFULLY cold, lasting for weeks, but Morag kept at it, wondering when these last remaining kelpies would tire of chasing her. She was certainly tired and ready to settle down somewhere quiet, though both her arm and her wing had regained some strength from all her flying.

Most of the kelpies had finally lost interest or—she hoped—gone back to the hidden realm. But the kelpie prince, the one who cared the most, was not giving up.

When Morag found a burn that led to where the water was thin and kingdom silver close to the surface, she made her final move. Only the kelpie prince followed her, and when it lay on the bank with its feet in the water, she slipped away in the night.

The hollow tree took some time to find again. After several passes, she spotted the cluster of snow drops with their outer floppy white petals acting as a beacon. *Thank you, Solly, for your years of pestering me with your flower knowledge.*

With steeled resolve, Morag reached into the hollow tree to grasp the magical bridle. She patted around but found nothing but moss. The hollow tree was empty. *Maybe it was a different tree? Nae!* She searched several of the surrounding trees, her heart racing faster by the second and frustration setting in. For a brief moment she thought the kelpies had found it, but nae. The prince would not still be following her if it were so.

Morag, how could you? She'd lost the one treasure Cadha had entrusted her with hiding. She'd let Cadha down. If only Solly or Mavis had taken the bridle, they'd know exactly where it was.

Emotionally worn out, Morag stopped her pacing and sat to rest. What was she to do? She couldn't keep the kelpie prince waiting too long or it would get suspicious. Of all the—Morag slowly grinned.

Cadha.

Cadha knew exactly what she had been doing. If Morag lost the bridle, then literally no one, not even herself, would know where it was. Clever queen.

Buoyed with renewed energy, Morag set off for the Tarner, eager to keep the remaining kelpies busy for as long as it took for the hidden heirs to grow up.

Acknowledgments

Some quick, but heartfelt thank you notes to friends, colleagues and beta readers who helped bring this book to fruition. In order of first look to last look: K. A. Bledsoe, who is always up for a "rough" read. Sarah Chanis, who was an early champion. Kitty Bucholtz for her insightful edit notes. Our beta readers Srishti Bansal, Hannah Bird, Sunshine Blevins, Kathy Brodie, Katie Class, Karen Jones, Keri K., Kristi Miller, and others: your keen eyes helped make the story flow as swiftly as the Tarner, but with fewer problems! And lastly, Lisa Knapp, whose proofread pass put such a nice polished shine on things. Any remaining typos or plot inconsistencies, are mine, because even after I write this sentence, I'm probably going to go back and read the book one last time and tweak one more thing.

Thank you ladies for your diligence, sharp eyes and minds, and the great care you took with this story. I'm so grateful for you!

BOOK 1: RISE OF THE KELPIES

A girl meant to be a pawn starts playing her own game.

Almost twenty years after the Kelpie Wars, Farrah's world is upended when a river kelpie invades her remote village and kills the hidden prince she was supposed to be protecting. As a member of the secret society created during the Kelpie Wars, Farrah knows she'll be asked to pose as the prince's twin sister and carry out the Society's plans to safeguard the kingdom.

So, when the palace's attention turns to finding the missing princess, Farrah travels to the capital with hundreds of other orphans also claiming the crown. She is more interested in finding justice for the prince than she is in becoming the princess. And when tragedy strikes along the way, Farrah will have no choice but to fight for those she loves.

Rise of the Kelpies is a cozy fantasy fairy tale in which a girl trying to save her kingdom has to learn to trust. Read *Rise of the Kelpies* and travel to Glenmoor Kingdom, a magical place with rebellious palace fairies and dangerous river kelpies.

ALSO BY SHONNA SLAYTON

Which one will you read next?

Fairy-tale Inheritance Series

Cinderella's Dress

Cinderella's Shoes

Cinderella's Legacy (novella)

Snow White's Mirror

Beauty's Rose

Sleeping Beauty's Spindle

The Little Mermaid's Voice

Lost Fairy Tales Series

The Tower Princess

River Kelpies Series

The Queen's Hidden Legacy (prequel)

Rise of the Kelpies

Reign of the Kelpies

Historical Women

Liz and Nellie: Nellie Bly and Elizabeth Bisland's Race Around the World in Eighty Days

Lessons From Grimm

Lessons From Grimm: How to Write a Fairy Tale (Writer's Guide)

Lessons From Grimm: How to Write a Fairy Tale Workbooks Series

Writing Prompts From Grimm (Story-starter Series)

ABOUT THE AUTHOR

SHONNA SLAYTON visited her first castle in grade four and was hooked on history forevermore. With so much scope for the imagination, writing about both fairy tales and history seemed a good fit. Her first series, the *Fairy-tale Inheritance Series* is rich with tales of family heirlooms, hidden secrets, and, of course, fairy tale magic.

She grew up in British Columbia and now lives with her husband and children in Arizona.

To stay in touch and learn about new books, be sure to:

Join her newsletter at: ShonnaSlayton.com

Visit her store (USA) at: ShonnaSlaytonBooks.com

www.ingramcontent.com/pod-product-compliance
Lightning Source LLC
Chambersburg PA
CBHW021716190726
48289CB00008B/2555